THE VISIONS
of
CARADOC

THE VISIONS
of
CARADOC

———

Tom Davies

AZURE

First published in Great Britain in 1999 by
Azure
1 Marylebone Road
London NW1 4DU

British Library Cataloguing-in-Publication Data

A catalogue record for this book is available from
the British Library

ISBN 1 902694 01 5

Typeset in Bembo and Benguiat by
Pioneer Associates, Perthshire
Printed in Great Britain by
Caledonian International Ltd, Glasgow

Contents

———

A SUNSET COMMUNION

The sun dipped out of the Valley at the end of the long, autumnal day, burnishing one of the furthest peaks so brilliantly a passing angel might have dropped its halo right there.

There was the luxuriant sound of Tchaikovsky on the radio in my allotment shed and, after an hour of light weeding, I went and stood by the fence looking out at that dropped halo of light.

A stray sheep cried out in the thickening darkness and my nose picked up the wafting smell of woodsmoke. My hands were dirty as I placed them on the hard creosoted fence and, if anything, that dropped halo became larger and more luminously brilliant.

In the beauty of this given moment I saw the whole of my Valley as one vast cathedral with the lights of the nearby houses looking like stained glass windows. The river running the length of the Valley floor was the cathedral's nave and that place where the dying sun was washing over that peak was the high altar. The ceiling was a vast vault of sky nailed up there by many stars.

And there was Old Caradoc, a lone pilgrim with dirty hands, standing at a creosoted communion rail patiently waiting to be fed. Here was an old worker of the soil, with trouble with his legs, needing at that moment to be fed with the body of Christ.

So I found a bit of old bread in the snap tin in my allotment shed and there was an inch of wine left in a bottle too. The bread was stale and the wine was sour but I only needed a taste as I fed myself, reciting aloud those words which are engraved on my heart: 'Take and eat this in remembrance that Christ died for thee and feed on him in thy heart by faith with thanksgiving . . .'

Then, with Tchaikovsky still playing in my shed, I raised my arms in prayer on behalf of these ancient hills of coal, calling on God to be gentle with all of us and cleanse us of our sins. This was my moment here at the communion rail of the world; a time of personal worship and celebration.

The sun had nearly gone by now, leaving just a thin sliver of light as a hunting bat flitted overhead. There was the sound of a woman's laughter and someone was trying, but failing, to start a car. You could already feel the start of a big rush of night cold charging down the Valley slopes.

It is easy for us to look around the Valleys and believe that God has forsaken us. But he is always here and, at certain given moments, you can actually feel him all around you. At these moments we should all take the time for some personal worship and celebration.

There is a whole generation of my collier tribe here in my body. I am them just as surely as they are me and that was the way I joined my people with God at the end of that long autumnal afternoon. Everyone fed one another with the body and blood. We were all blessed and became as one in front of the high altar of a Valley home. Theirs was the kingdom, the power and the glory as an old man, who keeps struggling to maintain his faith, stood crying with tribal poetry at a sun which, sending up a new explosion of gold, seemed reluctant to leave the Valley.

A PRAYER CLEAN

Some like to jog and others to drink but I often like to walk through my village firing flash prayers at anyone and everyone I come across.

They never know what's going on, of course, but anything that moves will get hit by a flash prayer from Old Caradoc on such mornings when my mind will try and bring them into touch with the peace and love of God. A few will find themselves unexpectedly and mysteriously warmed and turn around with the most brilliant smile on their face. But most will continue on their dreary way of getting and spending without so much as a pause or a look back.

Prayer is the very first balm of all healing and I might find myself in the surgery waiting room trying to detect illnesses or wounds and firing my love darts at them. The milk man will get a hit and the committee chairman and the drunks on the park bench.

The ever-marauding sheep might cop a fusillade too as would

the local video shop on which, I know, it would be totally wasted. You could fire whole Springer missiles of prayer into those parlours of evil and they would just disappear into those hateful cassettes without so much as a whisper.

But the real trick of flash prayers, I believe, is to imagine the whole skeleton of the community and then keep firing off bursts at the sick joints: at the police station and the Welfare Hall where all the drunks are singing 'My Way'; at the little council estate where so many of the youngsters seem to be graduating in burglary and at the shop where people are weekly maintaining their pulverizing greed with their Lottery tickets.

You could almost divide up the whole community with prayer lines, quartering it again and again as you swamp every single lost corner in believing prayer. There's the house where the father has just cleared off; here's the doomed home of all those druggies. Hey, catch that kid with the bandaged finger and that woman almost bent double with arthritis. Whitewash the whole lot with prayer.

Yesterday I caught almost half the village from the old dead pit down to the school. Tomorrow – God and my own wobbling legs a'willing – I'm hoping to work my way through the other half.

Some of my own prayer walks have been amongst the most invigorating and joyful that I've ever taken, particularly on sunny mornings when you can close your eyes as you pray, turning your face to the sun and feeling a sort of celestial blaze in your brain.

Then you can just turn loose whole glittering lariats of prayer and keep them whirling around and around your head. Soon you are directing this prayer and getting it to swoosh through walls and windows and closed doors where they can bring comfort to the broken and dry a few tears. With enough believing prayer around the place all our troubles would come to an end.

There's never enough believing prayer around, of course, but, on mornings like this, Caradoc does what he can. God's very electricity comes alive in believing prayer. Prayer is at the very heart of The Mystery of the Cross.

I pray at and for my people; I carry them up to the wounded heart of God with the quiet plea that they will there come to examine the condition of their own heart.

So, with Easter approaching and the very earth already stirring with promises of the resurrection, I urge my people to walk out in their communities and fire off fusillade after fusillade of flash prayers. Beseech God to help his stumbling, divorcing, sinful, drunken flock that they might find a path of healing and love out of their self-imposed barbed-wire wilderness.

Walk down your main streets slowly. Get them squarely in your sights and fire your love darts. If it moves hit it. Don't, on any account, miss anyone at all.

PULPIT SOAP

I don't suppose there is anyone at all from here to Treherbert who is not worried about television and the centrality it has assumed in all our homes and lives.

The dominant force and shape of our Valley culture used to be the pulpit in which great preachers with words of fire hammered out our very souls. The pulpit made us the big-hearted and magnificent tribe we once were; it was the very platform of all philosophy, poetry and drama.

These extraordinary preachers woke us up with the thunder and lightning of their personalities; their visions taught us how to be free and happy in the love of the Lord and, occasionally, they gave us a glimpse of true greatness. With their electrifying insights into the devastating nature of sin on the human per-sonality and their brilliant mastery of destructive definition, they were our first social engineers. They were the fathers of us all.

Well, television has clearly become our social engineer and father now; the box in the corner has become the new platform of all poetry, philosophy and drama which almost certainly explains why we are in such a complete mess. We become what we see, said the prophet. Truth has stumbled in the streets. The voices of criminals, murderers and rapists are being heard in every Valley home.

Old Caradoc is not against all television. I especially like *Songs of Praise* and *One Man and His Dog*. I also like to watch rugby internationals but Mrs Caradoc hates rugby – and the noise I make while I'm at it – so I have to watch the games on my little portable down in my allotment shed where I am usually joined by my friend Bomber and we share a flagon of something and make as much noise as we like.

Mrs Caradoc is a good woman who has had a lot to put up with but she has lately become addicted to that soap *EastEnders* so I'm now spending more time than usual in my shed where I enjoy studying theology or puffing on my pipe and listening to the slugs munching my cabbages. (No pipes allowed in the Caradoc household either, I'm afraid.)

But imagine my dismay the other week when I got home to find Mrs Caradoc in a right old tizz because someone called Grant had kissed someone called Michelle in *EastEnders*. I mean to say, what could Caradoc care if this Grant had kissed this Michelle? But this tiny woman – my own wife! – really was up in the air about it, going on and on about that poor, confused Michelle being kissed by that nasty, ugly Grant. I should write to the BBC about it and complain about the sheer unfairness of it all.

I carefully sniffed about but I don't think she'd been hitting that sherry again when I realized, with a cold shaft of insight, that television had taken over the Caradoc household too. The truth had stumbled in my very own parlour. Even the Caradocs had been sucked into this nutty East End fantasy.

Maybe those preachers of old in their pulpits of fire had a biblical line on whether Grant should have kissed Michelle. But I don't. I mean to say, they're a married couple, aren't they? But before Grant starts kissing anyone else, I am very tempted to sacrifice good old *Songs of Praise* and throw our television set on the local tip.

There's sure to be a very big war between the Caradocs if that happens and, if you knew Mrs Caradoc the way I know Mrs Caradoc, you would know that I am not bound to be the victor.

THE BIGGEST CHAPEL OF THEM ALL

When I was young our whole family sat beneath the pulpit of a preacher whose heart was in the right place but who also, it was generally agreed, was a bit of a dead loss.

On some Sundays his sermons could make your nose bleed with boredom but his other major quirk was that, prior to every Welsh rugby international, he would publicly plead with the Lord that Wales should be fed with the bread of heaven of an unbelievable number – nay, a cricket score – of points.

Sometimes he got us all down on our knees sharing in this same plea although, of course, we now know that this is a bad prayer and even worse theology. His chapel, I believe, was one of the first in the Valleys to be turned into a carpet warehouse.

But in one sense he was on the right track since rugby, religion and politics once formed an interwoven poetry in the Valleys which then projected our highest aspirations and ideals. The Arms Park became, for a lot of us, the biggest chapel of them all; a place of collective worship where our scarlet warriors offered our tribe dazzling visions of glory as they tore apart the Scottish, Irish or, with any decent luck, the English.

These men were our heroes who were also the standard bearers of our honour and faith. When they put on the sacred scarlet jersey we were there at their sides, not necessarily looking for a cricket score of points, but that they would represent us with passion and pride; that they would keep getting up and returning to the attack. The game was also first and foremost about fellowship – as was the chapel.

I was with my friend Bomber on that day when Phil Bennett scored that try against England after running the length of the pitch and Bomber remains the only man I have ever flung my arms around and kissed full on the lips. I do hope Phil doesn't score another, Bomber kept spluttering because it was his first time too.

But just look at this miserable bunch of whingers we now call a Welsh team. All they do is moan about money and there's not one of them who seems to want to move an inch unless he's sponsored. I just can't tell you how low my heart sinks when I see one of them opening a sports shop or a supermarket or selling perfume. Now for the incomparable honour of representing Wales they want wages. Wages!

Old Caradoc keeps on having a dream that Wales will collectively re-invent herself one day and become a great and dangerous nation again. But we need real icons for this and the Welsh team was a real icon in whom we invested our most beautiful ideals. But not anymore we don't.

We desperately need a team that will carry us as a nation and honour ancestral voices. We want them to renounce all taint of money and become ambassadors for our faith. We especially want them to be real and honourable men who, in the way they think, speak and play, are always pleasing to Wales and the God who, albeit with tears in his eyes, still watches over us all.

A WAFER OF MEMORY

It is important that we continue live acts of collective worship because this is virtually the only way we can enter into our past, engage with our nationhood and come close to our ancestral roots.

These are the doors that open up to us when we come together on our knees before the altar or when we use the liturgy or, even more importantly, when we eat that communion wafer and drink the wine.

Marcel Proust, in his giant masterpiece, *A la Recherche du Temps Perdu,* tells of a moment in adulthood when he eats a madeleine cake he first tasted as a child. This taste sets off a flood of memories, including the death of his grandmother, which he experiences for the first time, recalling her physical presence and grieving over her terrible absence.

The act of writing this book, then, brings all the chaotic fragments of memories together; we enter many of Proust's joys and pains; we feel the ebbing and flowing tides of love; we open the door into the secret essence of his being and we actually come to inhabit his frail, raffish humanity.

This, in a way, is what happens to us when we come together to worship. We are opening the doors into our collective past and racial memories, we are taking in moments of triumph in love and war, we can even relive the pain of our darkest hours when God seems to have withdrawn from us totally – as on the morning of the Aberfan slide.

When Old Caradoc takes the communion wafer he might even be Marcel Proust tasting again that madeleine cake, often feeling his tribal imagination borne up on an intricate magic carpet woven with mine disaster, Whitsun joys and cold hostile winters of hardship and strike. These memories might later start gusting particularly strongly in the singing of hymns which in themselves can take me anywhere from the side of an open grave on a rainy morning to the terraces of the National Stadium just prior to the kick-off of an important rugby international.

These memories unfold randomly, the one making an unfamiliar connection with the other until they begin stretching back through the century and even beyond that. They unfold like a river which dawdles in places but then moves into fast flood before slowing to a summer trickle again, all moving through the landscape of the Celtic imagination which, rather like a glacial valley, was first sculpted by the endless interplay of worship, hymn and prayer.

It is possible in worship, then, to walk back into the history of Wales and be at the side of the Rebecca rioters or sit with Bishop Morgan as he worked on his translation of the Bible. Anything is possible when the memory releases the Celtic imagination and the point of the journey, of course, should be that we ultimately end up sitting at the table where Jesus broke bread with his disciples at the Last Supper.

When we worship and take the communion wafer we are entering into the full history of our spirituality which, in a sense, began at the table of the Last Supper. We are making our sacred past live again and joining ourselves to our ancestors. These are the acts of the imagination which can make religion a truly exciting adventure. These are the marvellous doors to new perceptions which can open in liturgical worship.

We might also recall that the whole of the Bible was remembered and passed on. Not one word was written down at the time of those earth-shaking events.

Everything we know about the life of Christ came down to us through memory and it is this memory which continues to bind us to The Cross today in precisely the same way as it began doing two thousand years ago. Memory binds us to one another. Memory imprisons us in our frailty and vulnerability. Within this memory we flourish as the wild, happy flowers of God.

When he took the bread and broke it Jesus said: 'Do this in

remembrance of me.' Memory is the way we establish a covenant with God, binding on him and us.

JURASSIC CARADOC

It has been a depressing week in the Caradoc household since more than a few people have been taking the mickey out of me, actually accusing me of not being 'with it'. One of my nephews even had the temerity to refer to me a Jurassic Caradoc.

Such taunts and insults pain Old Caradoc deeply since he has long taken a great pride in being very much 'with it' and has always been careful and diligent in trying to keep up with all the latest literary and musical trends.

Oh, all right, I know my clothes aren't exactly of the groovy nineties and there are often outbreaks of hilarity in the knitting circle when they spot my sock suspenders. And, yes, I do like my ancient pin-stripe suit with matching waistcoat and gold fob watch. But I've practically lived in that suit all my life and, apart from my birthday suit, it's the only suit I feel really comfortable in.

Yes, yes, I also do like to wear a butterfly starched collar but they're the only collars I've got and Mrs Caradoc did buy me a new, forget-me-not blue shirt a few years back but it's still in its David Morgan wrapper.

Now, on the question of music, it is true that I like to listen to a lot of choral stuff on my vast collection of old 78s but I also like to listen to the Ted Heath Orchestra. But there really is nothing remotely Jurassic about Old Caradoc since I also have something called a tape cassette player and I did once pick up a tape of *Jesus Christ Superstar* in the bargain bucket in Woolworth's.

Sometimes I play this for Bomber down in my allotment shed and I have to report to you now that it's not bad. In the business they call it a 'rock opera' and it is about the last seven days of Christ with lyrics by Tim Rice and Andrew Lloyd Webber.

This pimply twosome have the sublimest musical and lyrical gifts and there's an overture full of motifs in the best bel canto and Broadway manner and an instrumental Crucifixion passage of sustained quarter-tone pitches with Tristano-type piano figurations constantly overlapping. Or something.

Bomber and I particularly like to sing along with 'I Don't Know How To Love Him' or, Bomber's favourite, 'King Herod's Song'. There is also a lot of lovely string and choral writing in this opera and the only pity is that Bomber's voice – even when he's had a couple of drinks – sounds like a rope under the door.

I have also enjoyed a few of the Beatles' records, particularly that marvellous 'Satisfaction', even if some of Martin Lennon's remarks about Christ were a bit iffy to say the least. Steven McCartney still seems a nice enough sort and Ringo is, well, just Ringo. The Rolling Stones are good at strutting their stuff too and few in the church will write anything as deep and touching and true as their 'All You Need is Love'.

So you will deduce from all this, I hope, that Old Caradoc is, in point of fact, very much 'with it' even if, in literary matters, he does, it is true, tend to be slightly behind the times. Just at the moment I am reading – and greatly enjoying – a collection of Celtic night prayers. Groovy. Last week I re-read Thomas à Kempis' *Imitation of Christ*. Absolutely fabulous.

But someone out there has recently sent me a copy of *Trainspotting* with the clear intention of winding me up. And I think I know who it is too and he had better watch his step or he is going to get pilloried in this pulpit every week from now until next Christmas.

This 'book' was somehow written by someone while he also had his head down a lavatory pan. It is one long scroll of unimaginable filth and, just on the evidence of the first page, it will never, I confidently predict, replace writing.

Yet if this really is popular and current art I had better say right now that, far from impressing you all with my grooviness, Old Caradoc, far from being with it, is, in fact, proud to be well and truly without it.

OUR POOR DEAD KIDS

It is now an article of absolute faith, that, when it comes to a talent for fantasy and self-deception, the people of South Wales must be Olympic gold medallists without a challenger in sight.

There is a lot of worry in the Valleys these days about the drug problem and, as yet another young body is carted away with a needle still dangling out of his arm, you hear the same old voices in the terraces complaining about how the young have gone to the dogs.

But at almost any hour of the day you can also hear these same old voices ordering drinks in the clubs and pubs; buying their favourite bottles of spirits in the off licences or down on their knees in front of the doctor pleading for yet another ton of valium or temazepam because they can no longer face reality in any shape or form.

Every level of the Valleys is sodden with some form of drink or drug; the flight from reality is complete and there is barely anyone who is not on something as they stumble around like dribbling robots complaining, when they get words out at all, about the young. It never occurs to these fatheads to look into the mirror for one second.

Jesus took no hard line on drink; he made the finest wine and, when it ran out, he made some more. Even Old Caradoc has been known to take a drink or three but we were always taught about the perils of excess and yet it is the regular and excessive abuse of every drink and drug going which has now reduced my people to lying flat on their faces in the gutters of their own self-pity where they blame everyone from John Major to the neighbour's dog for the way the roof has fallen in on their lives. Everyone except themselves.

Drink and drugs are poisons which promote only selfishness. They have long destroyed the faith of my people just as surely as they are now destroying every home, family and relationship. Love is a totally alien, if not impossible, notion for a drunkard who is only ever capable of sitting in a corner wondering where his next drink is coming from. He can never act lovingly because he is incapable of love; he is literally imprisoned in his own cant and self-deceit. A drunk is a totally pointless object.

Oh aye, it may well be that the drugged young are going to the dogs but it is the drunken old who have taken them there. Let's not try and wriggle our way around that.

The Valley communities may yet repair their broken bodies by purging and cleansing themselves in the power of the Holy Spirit. They may even yet awake from their drunken and drugged dreams but, as a first step, they must discover the old-fashioned yet important virtue of sobriety. They should also remember that they are their brother's keeper and that the poor dead kid with the needle in his arm is their own poor dead kid. They set the example and so the blame for his premature death should be laid nowhere else but squarely at their drunken doors.

A RAINBOW OVER ABERFAN

I pulled up in my little car on the Valley road the other day and saw something which both warmed my heart and brought tears to my eyes. I saw a rainbow over Aberfan. It curved right up out of the valley in a coloured arc of truth but, even in my tearful joy, I could still see that grim, grey morning of mists when that tip exploded and came crashing down on top of that school killing 116 children and 28 adults.

Old Caradoc was there on the morning of the rescue; he entered as deeply as anyone into the suffering of his people. The name Pantglas has since been carved in blood and pain on all our hearts.

Next week marks yet another anniversary of that fateful morning whose every detail I still carry with me as closely and intimately as the secret dust in the linings of the pockets of my suit. That was the morning which shook and almost destroyed my lifelong faith; that was the morning that destroyed a lot of my people's faith.

Even nearly 30 years later many a Valley heart still brims with a bitterness with God for allowing such an obscene event to happen. This bitterness is even carved on some of the tombstones of the children's graves in the cemetery. I would never speculate on the mind and thoughts of God because he does not think as we do but I do now believe that we can see this terrible disaster as both an opportunity and a hope.

Instead of thinking of the Aberfan disaster as an epitaph on the lives of these poor children, we should come to see it as an altar at which we dedicate the lives of all our Valley children today. We should use the lives that have been lost as an inspiration to take hold of the lives of our young now. Those that have perished will then be seen to have reached out and passed on the flame; they will not be seen as having died in vain.

The real trouble with our faithlessness is that we no longer care for our young as they stand around staring in through the empty windows of the Job Centre with a bucket of glue in one hand and a kung fu video in the other. And not only do we not care about them, we are also afraid of them; we merely lock our doors and hope they will not burgle us.

This faithlessness also means that we do not have the will to provide them with any shelter from the gusting monsoons of crime and unemployment which are sweeping the Valleys. We are not angry on their behalf; we are not raising our fists and shouting for them. The young are lost because we are lost too.

So as another anniversary of our greatest heartbreak approaches we should make the day an altar on which we stand crying out on behalf of our young. The loss of one generation should not lead to the loss of the next.

There were tears in my eyes when I saw that rainbow over Aberfan because I took it to mean a possible resurrection of the spirit of this lost and faithless collier tribe of mine. I also took the rainbow to represent the throne of Christ who will one day return to this blighted land and gather the young around him and make their lives new.

A MESSAGE OF HOPE

I normally wake in the middle of the night, often with my arms and legs riddled with the pains of old age, but the other night I opened my eyes and actually heard joyous hymns and jubilant voices of prophecy. There was also a dazzling halo floating through the darkness.

But I was very calm since I knew that God had been reaching out to touch me again as he has so often done in the past so, without even thinking, I welcomed him in tongues which is how I always speak to him when I am not quite sure what to say.

I almost immediately understood that this visit was a message of hope. God was telling me that he would never allow catastrophe to be the final word and that he didn't want Old Caradoc to just keep singing funeral songs over the body of his stricken people. There had to be hope too.

Such messages are well known to those religious people with a penchant for gloom; they are the means by which a creative God often revives the optimism of his followers; an earnest of his willingness to keep intervening in a world whose very heart is being eaten away by the relentless and predatory forces of evil.

At one stage I had to raise my hand to shield my eyes from the dazzling glow of that floating halo which then sank directly into my body, taking away all my pains and giving me such a strength that I felt I could have taken a shovel and re-opened the local dead pit single-handedly.

The real focus of all Christian hope, of course, is the return of the Son of Man who will then restore all our failing strength and dry all our despairing eyes. The faithful have long believed in The Return implicity: there are 318 references to The Second Coming in the New Testament. It is Christ's greatest and most repeated promise: 'I will not leave you as orphans' (John).

The times feel right for this final move too. Social stability is collapsing. Our children are being attacked like no other generation and our teachers are being stabbed in the streets. We are also witnessing events which the Bible teaches would be consistent with The Second Coming. Christ will return when there are wars and rumours of wars; when there are famines and earthquakes, it is written down. St Paul told us of the moral traits of the last days . . . love of self, love of money, boasting, arrogance, disobedience to parents, ungratefulness, lack of self-control, hatred of the good. There will also be revival in interest in demonic activity (Timothy) and the stockpiling of riches (James).

So the stage may well be set for the final great battle between good and evil; a time when all moves to drive God from his throne will fail miserably and the massing clouds of evil will be firmly and finally repulsed by the transcendent brilliance of The Second Coming.

And so it was that a night vision had made an old man's faith new again. He had been handed a candle of hope in the darkness and continued lying there until he heard the milk being delivered and all the other sounds of his Valley community coming awake.

Yet with the dawn those terrible pains came back into my arms and legs too, reminding me perhaps that all things must pass and that while the time of The Return may be soon, it will not be just yet.

IDRIS THE POINTLESS

There was a nice young lad who lived at the end of the next terrace and got us all worried when, around the age of thirteen, he began wearing safety pins through his nose and dyed his hair a forget-me-not blue.

He also began reading strange paperbacks by even stranger American writers and everything took a decided turn for the worse when he then went to art school down Cardiff way where he began producing a range of disgusting canvases. Meet Idris the Pointless.

When Idris came home the other week on a mid-term break I was rather surprised when he called in to see me as I was brooding in my allotment shed. We hadn't spoken for a long time but this Van Gogh in safety pins asked me if I thought there was such a thing as Christian art and, if so, what was it?

It was a good question which got me humming and haahing a bit since, although I certainly do believe that there is such a thing as Christian art, I've never believed that a Christian artist was obliged to dot his work with such things as crosses, visions or angels. A Christian artist should show his faith in his world view.

Most modern artists declare their loss of faith when they keep courting violence, darkness and horror, I told Idris. They hold up a mirror to the world with their camera, pen or paintbrush and then distort it with their own sick obsessions which they have, almost without exception, picked up from the work of other artists. This infection is so widespread there is now hardly an original star in the whole firmament of art.

A Christian artist, on the other hand, would generally seek to affirm that which is pure, good and lovely. He would always be seeking to mediate the beauty of the ordinary world to us; he would be looking for new insights into reality and, in this way, celebrate the fantastic wonder of creation.

The Christian artist would never bother with a pervert, preferring to study a normal man at work or play; he would never gaze at a scene of horror when he could find a real moment as it floats, like a falling leaf, through the real world. The art of the Christian is the most difficult art of them all.

We have lost sight of God because our artists have lost sight of God, I went on. These artists no longer believe in the value and beauty of the ordinary world because they no longer believe in themselves; they have succumbed to the unchristian notions of alienation, rebellion and despair.

When, yet again, you see yet another violent and foul-mouthed film which insists that it is 'telling it like it is', all you are really seeing is the work of yet another derivative artist who has lost his faith. But the real tragedy here is that, as long as they keep telling their lies about the world, then they keep attacking that world; they keep bringing the lie that little bit closer to the truth as they keep poisoning the fallen body of that world.

So there was clearly a challenge for any young artist here, so why didn't Idris face up to it?

Well, interesting as all this was, Idris the Pointless didn't have any more time to stay here gabbing with me in my shed since he was hard at work on a new project. Painting portraits of the homes of all the convicted murderers in the Valleys, he said. Yes, it often really is better to talk to a brick wall.

DEATH BY LAUGHTER

If there is one thing that often chills my old bones when I look around me it is the sight of many of my Valley people who give every impression of being engaged in some vast and suicidal enterprise of laughing themselves to death.

There are the foul, racist jokes of such as Bernard Manning (laughter); a child has fallen off a swing in Jeremy Beadle's *You've Been Framed* (more laughter); the local Post Office has been broken into again (even more laughter) and the windows of the local police station have been smashed (laughter unconfined).

This urge to laugh in the face of our most serious menaces is going to rip all our lives apart as surely as crime and violence. Just standing there laughing at reality is not going to help us free ourselves of our growing fear. It is simply not possible to laugh our problems away although such laughter will certainly make them a good deal worse.

The Nazis deliberately manipulated the entertainment industry to keep the people cheerful. 'See to it that the Germans learn to laugh again,' said Hitler. The Germans were then fed on a diet of anti-Semitic jokes with one of the consequences being that six million Jews were murdered in cold blood while the German people merrily carried on laughing themselves to death.

Christ wept often enough but he never laughed. He wanted us to take his ideas seriously and unambiguously; he didn't want to leave us with the opportunity of dismissing his words as mere jokes. But, that said, his was a ministry of joy; a celebration of the act of creation in which we have all since been joined together with laughter in our hearts. His ministry became a continuous river down through time which has both healed and restored while also setting itself squarely against the gathering clouds of evil.

Laughter, it should be clear, is one of our most precious gifts and a capacity to laugh is one that distinguishes us from animals. Laughter can be a high art form which can tell us much about freedom, often taking the poison out of an oppressive situation.

When a Christian laughs he is saying that the facts of the world are not the end of the matter; he is joining in with God's own laughter and delight in his creation. Laughter heals and can set up a ferociously democratic theatre which can bring us all together as one.

The Christian also knows what it's like to be laughed at; he knows what it is like to follow a much-mocked man who died on a cross to taunts and sneers with a sign over his head lampooning his laughable claims. The Christian probably understands more than most about the various ironies, parodies and mockeries that come with laughter.

But what everyone should know – whether they are a Christian or not – is that there are times to laugh and times to weep; there are times to be serious and times to have fun. Some issues are emphatically beyond jokes and if, for example, we are not all going to be swept away by this swelling tide of crime and violence, especially here in the Valleys, we should all get deadly serious about it and stop standing around as we sink up to our knees in these new and destructive waves with just a dirty joke on our lips and our heads full of empty laughter.

Despised lone mums

I've been suffering from a weary sense of *déjà vu* lately as I've been watching this odious and disgusting government lining up the guns and focusing their sights on single parent mothers. I'll repeat that. *On single parent mothers!*

That was something the po-faced bigots of the old chapel movement used to do so well earlier this century: denounce some poor young pregnant girl in the pulpit and then ostracize her from the 'right-thinking' community for the rest of her life.

We've got a bit more advanced than that these days and a compassionate church would now only say 'Oh dear' but then continue to protect – and fight for – these girls and their babies with all her power. Who among us has not fallen for someone we shouldn't have? Every single one of us lives in a glass house; our human weakness and vulnerability make us what we are.

When Mary became pregnant with Jesus there was an early suspicion that she was a single parent mother until that angel appeared to Joseph with the news. In the excessively puritanical Jewish society of the time Mary would have attracted a lot of sneers and nudges. 'Oh so it was God was it?' Mary would also have known all about the pain of rejection by the 'right-thinking' community as she lay struggling to give birth on that stable floor.

But Jesus grew up to become a friend of the powerless and an enemy of the powerful; he took the weak and vulnerable under his wing and even had a despised tax collector in his gang. He set out to heal society's wounds with a compassionate heart and a basic doctrine of forgiveness. Let's never forget the centrality of forgiveness to his whole life and work; if Christianity is not about forgiveness it's about nothing at all.

We know for certain that Jesus would have been absolutely horrified by this current crop of cruel and hateful politicians who seem to believe that the basic duty of every member of society is to turn a profit. We can somehow see him storming into the House of Commons and kicking over the Mace in angry protest at these politicians' appalling inhumanity.

Wild horses wouldn't have dragged him out again either, and we can even, with no small stretch of the imagination, feel his blistering fury at this proposed attack on the helpless and their babies.

Political robots like John Redwood who talk of cutting off the state benefit to these young girls can know nothing about them. These girls are not brain surgeons but they have kept their pride and look after their babies well. They would also rob and steal for their children if they were forced to and who would blame them for that?

Unusually they could even then burgle our houses with a moral justification. Even an old chapel dinosaur like me would break into the Bank of England rather than let one of my children starve to death.

So it rather looks as if we are going to all end up suffering even more than we're suffering now. As these mothers became more desperate, then we're all going to become more desperate, staggering and stumbling as we already are in the Valleys in this long, slow blizzard of crime, unemployment and violence.

These young girls are our young girls just as surely as their babies are our babies. They are all members of our family and should be cherished and protected as such. If these young girls are attacked by this outrage then it is up to us to defend them and a plague on all the Tory houses.

ASTROLOGICAL CLAPTRAP

It has always been the greatest marvel to me that my people are so often prepared to believe absolute rubbish. Education has managed to rid us of a lot of our dafter ideas but what is dafter – or more worrying – than the present fashion for astrology? If I weren't so mild-mannered and old I'm sure I would hit the next person who asks me: 'So what's your star sign, then?'

Even the staid old Abbey National is now offering their punters a booklet entitled *Your Astrological Guide to the Future* which should make for some good bedtime reading for all those in heavily mortgaged homes with negative equity.

Astrology is pseudo-waffle with no basis in science or fact. Not even the nuttiest astrologer has yet attempted to explain why stars billions of miles away affect our lives and futures. You are far more likely to be affected by that good smack from the midwife when you came out of the womb than the way Uranus was moving on Jupiter at the time.

I met a famous astrologer once while I was paddling in the sea on a Greek holiday. He invited me into his villa for a drink and, as he had to phone in his column within the hour, it soon became clear that he made it all up and right in the middle of a Greek brandy hangover too. No crystal balls, no charts, no nothing. Just another small Greek brandy and a big imagination.

But he was the clever one. We are the gullible saps who only swallow this claptrap because we don't know how to think properly.

Old Caradoc trained as a philosopher and he learned all that really needed to be learned from an old professor who sat in front of his essays like a huge woodpecker with a pince-nez, drilling every argument looking for weaknesses, examining every line and phrase and asking what it meant.

This professor alone would have destroyed all those wretched astrologers in five minutes flat. They would have all been hung at dawn. Nothing at all is worth saying if you can't also say what it means, was the one abiding lesson I learned from the old prof.

But the real menace of astrology is that it undermines faith;

it destroys the notion of an individual with free will who is in control of his own destiny; it denies the concept of an ordered, rational universe which works on ordered, rational lines. It also usurps the belief in a loving creator.

If my people ever re-found their faith in our loving creator then all their present crop of troubles would be over. If they ever set their minds on the study of the life and ideas of Christ, their whole blighted lives would be re-born anew. Faith is not some vague notion flying around the stars but something which works and heals and gives more life in the here and now.

But there is no sign of any revival in the faith of my people who continue to cling to their wretched Scratch Cards and consult their demented star signs. Crime will continue to tear their lives apart as they stand around helplessly watching their children become ever more evil in this season of ignorance and growing darkness.

So look again at those words about those handsome strangers and the way you might get angry but then regret it. They are the empty flannel that is going to be carved on your tombstone; they represent the mindless philosophy of an uneducated and faithless people busily making the dead march to oblivion.

SECRET BUNKERS OF PRAYER

So Christmas has come bearing down on us again like a runaway train and even as I write this late at night, three or four drunks from the club are involved in some sort of scuffling fight outside my front door.

At least they haven't yet actually urinated over my door as a few drunken punks managed to do about an hour ago. Just before that there were yet more carol singers yet again proving that they no longer know any of the words to any of the carols, and then of course there was the paper boy holding out his hand when he only ever gets my delivery right about once a month and that's by accident.

There's barely anything about the old Valley Christmas that I recognize any longer and, while there'll be the usual token crowd making their annual visit to the chapel on Christmas morning, I won't be among them since for about ten years now I have managed to get on a retreat in a Devon monastery from Christmas Eve to Boxing Day.

Christmas has long made me so gloomy that Mrs Caradoc is actually glad to get rid of me when I jump into my little car and make off to the monastery. At least she is then free to wallow in front of that hateful television in peace without me threatening to dump it down in the local tip. She even asked me the other day if I thought that Arthur in *EastEnders* would have to stay in the jug all over Christmas but I didn't rise to the bait. I could tell by her slight smirk that she was just trying to wind Old Caradoc up.

Anyway I'll have a swift half with my pal Bomber and then hit the road when, with a bit of luck, I'll arrive there just in time for supper. The place is Benedictine so we'll all eat in silence and then I'll fall as happily as a small baby into the monastic routine.

For here I feel almost immediately at home, addressing God's open wound of love in prayer. Here for a few days I can entwine my heart with his, taking us both down together to some secret place of the mind where the disgusting excesses and failures of the world celebrating Christmas are left far behind.

For a few days I am able to concern myself solely with my love relationship with God and my mind can sing healing love songs to his breaking heart. 'He prayeth well who loveth well,' Samuel Coleridge wrote.

Bells will then herald the start of Compline, that small and dark service of Gregorian chant in the candlelight which marks the end of the monastic day. Here all the terrors of the coming night are fully exorcized as the monks chant their goodnight prayers to God as they move around a single candle.

That first night of sleep is almost always my best night's of the year, making me ready for early Matins, another mixture of devotions and chanted psalms. The monks always don their hoods for this service, reinforcing the desired feeling of isolation and oneness with God alone. It is a service of psalms, hymns and scripture reading with voices which are both masculine but with a hint of abject melancholy.

Christmas Day is about the only day of the year when they

do not work tremendously hard, even if some of them do simply because they are so used to it and would, horror of horrors, have to sit around for a few hours actually doing nothing.

But they all know me and I exchange my news of the year with the same brother even if he usually has very little to tell me. I will also make a confession if the mood takes me. A full Mass is the centre of the day and for lunch there will be turkey and a little light banter but only ever a little. None of them ever really forgets – not even for a second – why they are all there.

Then with the approach of yet another night the atmosphere of the monastery seems to change and the robed monks take their places in the choir stalls, chanting and kneeling before God again, their black rounded shapes revolving around and dissolving into one another in the flickering candlelight. We are all of us of one mind and entering that mystical moment of worship again; praising God for the supreme gift and sacrifice of his only Son. This, for me, is the centre of a real Christmas; a time of love and worship which we have all long forgotten.

I have never yet understood what happens to me on my Christmas retreat in that monastery but I always return to the hungover Valleys feeling stronger, better and more hopeful. Those monks have become my partners in prayer; the ones who are always there to help me in my long, dark nights.

We should all be thankful that there are such monks at work in their secret bunkers of prayer. They are holy men giving God the prayer that he so loves to hear; they are beacons of hope in a world becoming ever more lost in its own long and ever darkening night.

LISTENING TO THE PAST

For a number of years now I have been the unofficial caretaker of a disused chapel which no one wants or worships in. One of the deacons once gave me a set of keys and, from that day to this, has never asked for them back.

I drop in there from time to time even though it is pretty much of a ruin with some scuffling rats beneath the floorboards.

But just walking into it is rather like putting on an old and much-loved glove since I grew up in this same chapel and know its every corner.

As a child I had a light soprano voice and I sang a number of solos on that altar. Our Sunday School class would gather in that corner there and just by here was where old Billy pumped the bronchitic organ. I kissed my first girl out on the back stairs but she didn't think much of the kiss and neither did her father when she told him about it.

But the jewel in the crown of this chapel was – and is – the pulpit where a succession of inspired and gifted men formed the mind and conscience of my people. Preachers made us what we are in that simple wooden frame and, about once a year, I still come here and varnish it carefully.

And there are also times when I will sit in the front pew and listen to the sermons and singing of the past. These sounds will come to me in a series of intensifications which might get louder and ever louder until they then fall away again into the roar of a passing car or the sounds of those scuffling rats.

Christmas Evans and Evan Roberts both once occupied this holy pulpit although that was long before my time. These great revivalists came to the Valleys as new Elijahs, catching a divine flash of lightning and using it to electrify and revive the souls of the Welsh.

They did nothing less than repulse a gathering darkness with the spirit of truth and, oh, how we all need to hear them again as the Valley communities sink ever deeper into a swamp of criminality, drugs and lies.

Everyone knows what a criminal culture is growing up around us but, far from telling the truth about it, their only response is to tell lies. They will not report the drug dealers; they accept stolen goods; they stand back and watch as roofs are vandalized or, even worse than that, they insist that all this criminality is got up by the media and is not there at all. Those old revivalists understood the restoring power of truth and they parented us in that understanding. But now look at the state of us!

Wales has had more religious revivals than any other country in the world and the faithful few often ask if we will ever see another revival but I can see no sign of it. Revivals are first and last gifts of the Holy Spirit. Nothing of any spiritual moment can happen without the Holy Spirit and even the greatest of our preachers have always been but its tools.

So I often just sit in my lonely and musty pew, looking up at an empty, newly varnished pulpit and do what any rational Christian can do: I beseech God in prayer that we may yet see another pulverising outbreak of the Holy Spirit throughout our Valley homes.

We must always keep a gambler's hope in our hearts and we shall never succumb to the redundancy of despair. God will, in the end, use the Holy Spirit decisively and powerfully. But the timing of such outbreaks will always be kept a secret, locked in his heart alone.

ROBOPREACHER

As it is now highly fashionable for anyone with a half-baked plan or thwarted ambition to apply for a grant, Old Caradoc has been thinking hard about putting in for one too.

It wouldn't be seemly for me to be seen asking for Lottery funds, after all the abuse I have poured on that disgusting operation, so I guess my application will have to go to Cadw, that strange and mysterious quango which seems to have been put there to cherish ancient piles of rubble.

Yet the ancient pile of rubble in question is not my disused chapel but my own failing body. You wouldn't believe all the various aches and pains I've been suffering from lately and it's got that Mrs Caradoc has got to bring up a pair of jump leads to get me out of bed.

So I've been thinking that, if old Cadw would give Old Caradoc a million or two, I could get everything replaced and become Robopreacher, punching the air with a plastic fist or thumping the daylights out of my new PVC pulpit.

But the point of such an important piece of restoration on such an ancient, if venerable, monument would be that I could then physically lay about these dozy churches and chapels of ours to try and raise them out of their historic and apparently endless slumbers.

No, I don't mean beating up the Archbishop of Wales, who is something of a sweetie and who once tried to write poetry, but actually getting out there and rolling up my sleeves in the thick of it, haunting their snoozing conferences and demanding, with my new, loud, amplified voice, that they finally learn how to make a moral stand.

Robopreacher's very first port of call would be the woodland outside Newbury where trees are even now being cut down to make way for some stupid and totally unnecessary bypass. And there, atop the highest tree, Robopreacher would rally all those great eco-warriors around him, calling on the sleeping Church to awake and side with them and also begin understanding how all roads tear apart our sacred environment.

The church should side with the poor, the dispossessed and the marginalized, they would hear from the top of this tree. The church should care about those who care and also understand the ravages of capitalism and the sure but steady way they are destroying our earth.

These hairy tree-lovers are precisely the sort of people that the church was first built for; outsiders who will not join this lemming-like rush to permanent gridlock; eccentrics who will not step forward and guzzle the national swill.

And yet, while these wonderful people were fighting for the lives of trees, the Church of England was holding a service in Coventry Cathedral celebrating the centenary of the car. The car! Well, at least they were celebrating it for a while until another equally wonderful woman took off all her clothes, letting her nakedness eloquently declare a pox on all the clergy and their rotten cars. They should have pinned a row of medals on her, though perhaps not.

A Decade of Evangelism was announced in 1990 but you would hardly know it. Such evangelists as we have couldn't convert a Jehovah's Witness and are all anyway probably too busy polishing their own cars. Indeed, the only time churchmen seem to get all interested is when it's something to do with this dysfunctional shambles they call the Royal Family. Next thing they'll be ordaining Fergie or something.

So, if you read a news item soon about a strange plastic figure perched up a tree in Newbury, calling on the church to start getting its act together, don't be too surprised. All it will mean is that the money has finally come through from Cadw to Caradoc and that, with all his many new bits, Robopreacher was launching his own Decade of Evangelism, ringing a wake-up bell on a thousand snoozing bishops and taking his message straight to those in the neighbouring trees; the great treasures of our society, the fighters who really matter.

A BAPTISM OF SNOW

The snow, when it comes as it did last week, is almost like a great annual act of re-decoration. One minute my village seemed shabby and even down-at-heel and next everything was made new.

Whole streets were covered in fitted white carpets with the terraces and pigeon coops all given their own made-to-measure white headgear. Rows of icicles hung off the gutterings and even the river froze to a beautiful, whorling standstill.

The broken-jawed pit managed to look lovely again too with all the nearby industrial debris covered by a foot of snow and just the old wheel-house poking its spindled, iron head up into the sky. Even the shattered old Welfare Hall managed to look spritely in its new white coat. Children got out their sledges and enjoyed themselves in the snow, rolling around in it and flinging snowballs at one another. People who found themselves without bread or milk talked to one another for a change and even helped one another as they always did in the old days.

On such mornings, with the fragrances of resurrection gusting around every corner, my very spirit gets up to dance and sing. This is a glimpse of our innocent and vibrant past. We have become a community again as we once were in the days of the miners' strike.

Snow always makes my memory re-enter those final days of the miners' strike when everyone battled so bravely and hard but then lost everything. General Winter brought in plenty of snow in those final days and up to a hundred villagers were out digging holes in the snow-covered sides of that tip and riddling up precious lumps of coal.

In the time of our direst need everyone came alive and looked out for one another. Old Caradoc always felt ten feet tall; he was so proud of his people and the way they conducted themselves; he felt so unbelievably honoured to be Welsh.

But the times of thaw after the snow are also interesting in the Valley where the sun always arrives late and leaves early. The morning sun clears one whole side of snow down to the river but the snow on the other side might stay there for weeks until it is finally cleared by rain.

Everything is one huge patchwork on the slopes in the thaw when you can also see sudden conjunctions of glittering light and it is even possible to catch the tail ends of angels as they whizz through the air and get on with their work. Angels are actually woven into the air but you can catch sight of them in luminous moments like this.

Many say that they do not believe in angels but that is only another symptom of our wholesale collapse of faith. It really is easy to believe in things invisible although, in times of snow and thaw, the work of angels always becomes highly visible – to Old Caradoc at any rate.

So say a prayer of thanks the next time you see a carpet of snow and try to hold your face up to catch the flakes. Feel them dissolve on your hot cheeks and think of them as the tiny kisses of angels who have come down from wherever angels live to re-decorate your place, revive a sense of community and bring innocent joy to the hearts of your cruelly threatened children.

Snow is a sign of God's willingness to keep offering a renewed contract to us; snow is the basic material which angels use for their work; snow is a communal baptism which, albeit briefly, turns us around and makes us all new.

BRILLIANT FIREWORKS

I can sometimes stand on the end of a terrace and see him shuffling towards me out of the Valley twilight. He has thick, caterpillar eyebrows and hard black eyes; he's got on his usual gangster slouch hat and then there's his talk except that this is not mere talk but a breathtaking flow of joke, hyperbole and epigram.

Gwyn Thomas is no longer with us, alas, but, when I need to, I can still get this intensification which brings him throbbing to life again; I can still warm my hands on the eternal radium of his humanity and humour. This man really will live forever and I see that one of his best plays, *The Keep*, will soon be shown on television. This wonderful play might be the only sensible reason to turn on a television set this year.

For Gwyn has become as rooted a part of Valley life as the coal they no longer want to mine here; he represents my people at their best and you can still, if you listen very closely, hear his immortal name being whispered by every stray Valley wind.

Old Caradoc bumped into him quite a few times over the years and, knowing my chapel background, he usually inquired cheerily: 'Ah, so how's God getting on today?' and I would always reply that God was doing just fine and certainly not losing any sleep over hard-nosed sceptics like him.

Gwyn was not one for the chapel, dismissing us as 'the chosen of the chosen', but that never seemed to affect our relationship and I anyway always thought him worth a charabanc-full of deacons. In fact I would have gone to him for help far sooner than anyone else I've known in the chapel. He had the steadiest and best of Christian virtues without so many of their vices; he was good and kind and without an ounce of malice.

He was also the authentic voice of the Valleys; a great comic commentator who always wrote memorably about life around here; 'This most improbable cocktail of music, laughter, drama and creative wit ever shaken by time, chance and inherited genes.'

He was the champion of the little, the underdog, the poor and the dispossessed. 'And then there was the obscenity of the mines; of men, you know, picked up in bits and taken home to his widow in a sack. It was the last great indecency.' His passion was nothing less than thrilling.

But those words, oh boy, those words: always majestic and brilliant in their flow. He once described Stanley Baker's daughter to me by saying: 'She just sat there with a smile on her face as if she had just rented the sun.' He was born in 1913 and 'the following year was even worse'. Richard Burton described him as probably the greatest talker in the world.

His wife, Lyn, was his greatest ally, driving him around, cosseting him like a mother hen and answering the phone because he would never touch the infernal thing. She could talk for Wales too and it was my personal theory that he got so good at talking by spending his whole waking life trying to get a word in edgeways.

When I called on him in his later years I found an ill man who was looking around him with an amused bitterness. The Welsh, he said, made him gloomier by the hour and that was a very exhausting business. 'It's these nationalists; they're the most marvellous organizers of a fuss.' Some say he died of neglect which is a common cause of death for any artist working in Wales.

I've always thought of him as one of the great Welshmen of our time, which is the reason for this eulogy. He may not have believed in God but God believed in him and he was anyway a god in his own right or, in his own inimitable words, he was: 'Potentially a saint and actually a heel . . . an error wrapped around a phoney gland.' No one writes like this any more.

So, whenever his loss becomes unbearable, I can stand at the end of the terraces that made up his world and, sooner or later, he comes to me again, with a smile on his face, a slouch cap on his head and yet more brilliant fireworks on his lips.

A HUNGER FOR VIOLENCE

Some time ago I told you of the huge and unquenchable appetite for violence which is the very engine of most American films and I further explained how biblical prophecy on a final tide of evil and lawlessness was clearly being fulfilled by the wholesale emergence of such films.

It has always been the most basic function of the Welsh pulpit to attack evil again and again; to expose its workings and call the attention of the people to its presence in their midst. This week I want to show another way in which this huge and unquenchable appetite for violence is wreaking destruction in our midst since I am going to explain how this same appetite for violence has made the tiny numbers of gangsters who call themselves the IRA what they are.

It is important to remember that the IRA are few in number, perhaps 50 and certainly no more than 100. There are more Eskimos in Ireland than there are active members of the IRA so how and in what way did this gang of thugs become so powerful and feared? Why does the BBC and ITV break into its programmes when they set off a bomb? Why do these men monopolize page after page of our newspapers and seize the headlines the world over?

These terrorists do this because they understand the evil at the heart of the modern media. These men have long seen and understood this huge and unquenchable appetite for violence of which I have been telling you and, having seen and understood it, they have been exploiting it mercilessly.

There is, these men know, no gain available in making speeches, writing pamphlets, going on demos or lobbying their MPs. All they have to do is set off a bomb and the whole global media will be putty in their hands because this same media loves nothing more than feeding off violence which is the media's basic and most irresistible food.

So when some young and callow youth from Wexford starts planting bombs in London the media does not simply report the plain facts in a few plain paragraphs, as it should do, but a feeding frenzy starts and there are special television programmes and bulletins, pictures of blasted buses and broken windows and pages and pages of waffling analysis. Everyone, everywhere is intimidated anew and this gang of thugs has won yet again. There are only three things the IRA has ever been interested in: publicity, publicity and publicity.

'Terrorism feeds off publicity,' Lord Annan wrote in his report on television. 'Publicity is its main hope of intimidating government and the public. The acts terrorists commit are each minor incidents in their general campaign to attract attention to their cause. By killing and destroying the terrorists are bound to extort publicity.'

The positioning of the Canary Wharf bomb tells us clearly about the way the IRA were thinking; set off a blast close to the new home of the newspaper industry; not close enough to hurt them but near enough to rattle their teeth and let them know the IRA were back in town.

This whole process describes the presence of aboriginal evil; it also points squarely to the future destruction of democracy and the way in which small groups with real or imagined grievances, seeing no point in talk or reason, will simply set off a bomb and, in so doing, be heard by everyone throughout the world through a supine media.

St Paul told us to think of whatsoever was pure, whatsoever was lovely and whatever men were of good report. 'Think on these and know God.' But our modern media thinks persistently on whatsoever is violent, whatsoever is ugly and whatever men are of evil report. Our modern media stands for the most part in unremitting opposition not only to God but to the most basic tenets of decency, elevating minor gangsters to major players with mythic powers.

We are all in far bigger trouble than anyone has yet imagined, if only because that trouble is largely being started by men in suits and with degrees who should know better. They are promoting a major evil, not only with their films but with a news industry which keeps dealing in a fear which is eating directly into all our hearts and minds. It is time all this madness stopped.

A WEEPING GOD

All my life I have had a stormy and passionate relationship with God to the extent that I have often quarrelled with him bitterly, cursed him and even, for many long years, run away from him altogether.

As a child I did what most chapel children did, which was to pay lip service to him in Sunday School, usually to get on the annual Whitsun Treat to Barry Island, when I also had the vague conception of him as a benign old duffer with a long beard who sat on a throne in the clouds.

But then one day, a few years after I graduated, he spoke directly to me and everything changed. My life, my ideas, my beliefs, my ambition . . . everything was shattered in a series of stormy visions which both shook me upside down and inside out while also giving me new insights into the world which then became the foundation of my life and work.

This was no benign old duffer, I then saw; this was a dazzling creative force beyond all human comprehension who was a law to himself and only like himself. This was a pure spirit of real feelings who inhabited the world and searched it for people to invade – as he had once invaded me – in the knowledge that they would then try and set out to extend his kingdom and make it a better place.

I ran away from him for many years, taking to drink and other women. Too much drink and too many women. But he hauled me back to him whenever the mood took him, encouraged me with quiet visions and explained to me his continuing and grave disappointment with his people.

Now that I am old and ill, with my wild oats long sown, we have an extremely easy and sunny relationship. I get no sudden and unwelcome bursts of his anger but, on some days, I go to the empty and near-derelict chapel in our Valley of which I am the unofficial caretaker and I sit there on the lonely pews and listen to the sounds of his overwhelming heartbreak.

He tells me of his pain at the sight of the long dead march of his people that he loves so much; he tells me of his anxieties about the cinema and the media; he complains much of the clerical bigots who speak in his name. But it's the future of the children in these lawless and sinful times that worry him the most.

He wants the Welsh to be at ease and happy with him again; he would love for them to start giving him the praise that was once the most abiding of all Welsh traditions. Sometimes, on my own in this old chapel, I do what I can either with a hymn or in tongues.

But, even as I sing, his heartbreak becomes almost unbearable and I falter and the praise dries up in my mouth as his weeping becomes as a monsoon and his heart keeps breaking like the snapping of so many pit props and he shows me all the valleys of Wales littered with dry bones. Yes, he shows me Wales as he sees it. 'Caradoc,' he says. 'Caradoc, will these dry bones ever get up and dance? Caradoc, will these dry bones ever again receive flesh? Will they ever again live?'

Such questions always become too much for me and I crash to my knees in bewilderment. 'Lord, Old Caradoc just doesn't know the answers to these terrible questions. He just does not know what the Welsh are going to do or how long they are prepared to suffer before they seek out your face again.'

Then the monsoon will stop and all the Valleys will disappear as I stand up again, not at all sure that I want to receive the burden of what I have been telling you. But he knows that I have this column, of course, and has long taken a lively interest in it. I can't truthfully say that there is much at all of me in these columns since he usually writes it, almost always in half an hour flat without a break or a word changed.

So Old Caradoc is being used yet again in this long dry season. He just stands alone with his God as they both look up out of the broken windows of a derelict chapel, both scanning the Valley skies for signs of rain.

⊕HE DEATH OF JONAH

And it came to pass that, on the eve of the Millennium, a wave of excitement rolled over the Land of the Wooden Spoonists since there emerged, from Tonyrefail, a young fly half called Jonah Cadwallader.

This Jonah was a youth of such outstanding rugby talents that he was, at the age of sixteen, made fly half for Wales. He had all the combined virtues of Jonathan, Arwel and Neil but none of their vices. Faster than Linford and built like a brick outhouse he captained a great defeat of Scotland and all the tribes of the Land of the Wooden Spoonists rejoiced mightily.

Big money offers came in from all parts of the world but Jonah was immediately signed to stay in Wales for all his sporting life by a complicated cash and sponsorship scheme which made him rugby's first multi-millionaire.

The actual terms of the deal were kept secret but it was understood by those in the know that he was to be paid a bonus of one hundred pounds for every point which he scored for his country and this sum would then be doubled as long as he never ventured into England to speak to an Englishman. If he did go as far as Gloucester – where a favoured aunt lived – it was only for one night a month in the company of three Welsh-speaking Welshmen and then back to Cardiff before midnight.

So far so good but the bob bank multitudes became slightly worried when they espied the logo of a bank on his boots, the logo of a soft drink on his socks, an emblem of an insurance company tattooed on his neck and the outline of a glass of stout on the patch over his nose. His spikey hair had also been re-modelled in the style of a logo for a well-known building society.

But the multitudes chose to ignore their inner worries and, lo, there was great excitement and the joy was unconfined when Wales took on England in the new National Stadium and Jonah ran in three tries in the first ten minutes. The sole Welsh strategy was to get the ball to Jonah and let him do the rest.

But then disaster struck when the whole English pack bounced Jonah off the pitch and he ended up with his building society head stuck in one of those revolving advertising hoardings. They pressed a button to get his head revolving out of it but it was the wrong button and Jonah came close to death since his head was now almost irretrievably stuck between an advertisement for cigarettes and another for condoms.

The full extent of his secret sponsorship scheme then became a little clearer when two ambulance men ran onto the field carrying a stretcher with two flaps dangling down on either side of it, advertising the advantages of a private health care scheme.

Jonah was then rushed to a private hospital where, as stated in his contract, he was duly opened up in front of the cameras from Sky television. They sent all manner of television probes up and down his veins and there was even an unconfirmed rumour that someone had spotted a miniaturized sign for Peter Alan estate agents of Penarth at the top of one of his arteries.

The emergency surgery on Jonah was deemed to be a complete success but, unfortunately, he never quite recovered conscious-ness. They even tried rattling bags of money in his ear for hours on end and, when this did not work, they tried reading out the winning sequences on the Lottery. But they had no luck with that either and after shouting a few words which sounded something like: 'I want more and Newcastle will pay it', Jonah Cadwallader duly kicked the bucket.

On the day of the funeral, when Jonah was buried in a coffin with the building society logo all over it, there was much lamenting in the Land of the Wooden Spoonists. Everyone wanted to know what had happened to the game which they had once loved so much; to this wonderful sport which had once carried the nation's highest social and religious ideals. Yes, the hungry sheep looked up and asked lots of questions but answers there were none.

THE MYSTERY OF LAWLESSNESS

I was listening to an interview with a director of a violent pornographic film on the radio recently when he uttered some words which made my blood run cold. 'I am only reporting truthfully on what's going on in the real world,' he said.

This, I suggest, is the lie of our time; this is the one persistent lie behind which all film directors hide and why we are all sinking into such a sorry mess. They used to say that the camera never lied but now it is clear that it never tells the truth.

First of all consider the medium and grammar of film; think of how they can now create monsters with computers; how a crowd of twenty can become a crowd of ten thousand; how night is turned into day and how they use plastic daffodils to create a spring or wood chippings to suggest snow. Suspects are interrogated in ten seconds; fugitives make fantastic and improbable leaps from one building to the next; people change into molten metal and back again. Everything is an illusion; it is a lie.

Old Caradoc once visited Universal Studios in Hollywood where we learned of false rain, of ice cream that was mashed potatoes and the revolving drum that was an earthquake. There was a huge set with a pond and a little man in a fishing boat on it. A huge shark reared up, frightening the kids and snaffling the man in the fishing boat. But this set had clearly just been built for visitors; even when they claimed they were going to tell us the truth behind the movie industry all they told was lies. Their characteristic posture is that of the pathological liar.

But, if we then reach into the hearts of these films to see how and in what way they report on the real world, what do we find? We find that, far from reporting on the real world, these film directors always go in pursuit of sensation and violence; they are always attracted to the criminal; they adore anything that is intense, melancholy or perverted. Nothing of the real world with real people resonates in their romantic work. Everything is a lie.

At the core of the Bible is the great mystery of lawlessness; a theological problem which generations of scholars have tried to unravel. This figure of lawlessness will come in the end times St Paul taught, and his arrival will be an essential precondition of the Second Coming.

Some have tried, unconvincingly, to argue that this biblical prophecy on the coming figure of lawlessness was fulfilled in the person of Caligula or then in Napoleon or even later in Hitler. But this mysterious figure has to be more than one person since, if you read the various references to this coming tide of evil carefully, you will see that it has to be a system which is global and even deceives the heads of nations and church leaders.

When he comes, St Paul said, he will come with 'all the powers and miracles of the lie'. He will claim our children and set himself up in every home. Everyone will be deceived and try to curry favour with him; a few will even worship him as he attacks even the mind of God.

I am sitting writing this in my beleaguered Valley home and can look out at the terraces which are covered with television aerials and satellite dishes. The windows of the shop have been smashed in again and another boy is feared to have died of drugs. Children I have long loved are turning into petty criminals and, with my heart turning over, I fear that the promised age of lawlessness is with us. I fear that the mind of the modern film industry, with its persistent lies, is nothing less than a major fulfilment of biblical prophecy and that we are all now beginning to see the terrible cost.

He is here, my people, criminalizing our children and destroying their basic moral framework without which they will not be able to lead honest and good lives. He is busy attacking us all and, unless we contain his lies, he is going to destroy us all inch by inch and hour by hour. Old Caradoc in his even older pulpit, a voice from the past, wants to know if there is any decency and fire left in the Welsh heart to resist him. Well, is there?

An EPIPHANY OF AGONY

Easter is the one time when the lost and wandering people of Wales should pause awhile and reflect that, just prior to the Crucifixion, Jesus was scourged.

The man would have been stripped and then chained to a post in a bending position when he would have been whipped with a leather thong studded with sharp bits of iron or jagged pieces of bone. These thongs stripped the skin from the backside to the extent that even the scourger's face would have been flecked with skin and blood. Most of those scourged fainted or went raving mad.

The man was given to the soldiers who had a great laugh giving him an old robe and a crude crown of thorns which cut straight into his scalp. He was also given a board covered in white gypsum; 'This is Jesus, King of the Jews', it mocked in black letters.

He was then taken to the place of his death in Jerusalem by the longest possible route, constantly jeered by the rabble and whipped on by the soldiers. He would certainly have been carrying the cross-beam since the custom was that the upright would already be there waiting for him.

Already weakened by many questions and whips Jesus would have staggered this way and that on his walk, helped only by Simon of Cyrene, a passing pilgrim. The others who loved him would have followed at a distance, including his mother who knew that he was about to give himself to mankind on a cross just as she had once on a stable floor.

At a place called Golgotha the cross was laid on the ground and he was stretched out on top of it. The practice was that a victim should be offered some relaxing wine but Jesus refused any. His body was mounted on a saddle half-way up the upright which would stop his hands being ripped off the nails.

— 38 —

As those crude nails were hammered into the middle of his palms he neither spat at nor cursed his executioners but prayed for their forgiveness. He was wearing only a loin cloth for decency and the soldiers gambled for his robe. Then the cross was lifted in an epiphany of agony and the crown of thorns would actually have moved in his pain-wracked brow.

From a height of about eight feet Jesus hung alone, reviled by his enemies. Ah, so this is the Son of God, well, if so, do something about it. Even the two villains on either side of him joined in the satirical banter until one asked to be forgiven and Jesus said one of the most astonishing lines in history: 'Today you will be with me in Paradise.'

Crucifixion was one of the longest and most lingering deaths ever known. A man might hang there for days and he would have had to keep moving his weight around to relieve the constant pain. He would be frozen by the night frosts, become raving through thirst or have his brains literally boiled by the ferocious sun. The wounds from the nails quickly brought on gangrene although the normal way of death would be for the lungs to rupture and for him to drown in his own blood. If a man still refused to die he was pounded to death by a mallet.

But fortunately they did not need to take a mallet to Jesus who, many say, simply died of a broken heart. 'It is finished,' he cried and died with a child's goodnight prayer on his lips. These words were the act of a man who had finally climbed a mountain and cried in delight that he had made it. The summit had been scaled. Nothing more could be done or added.

This man who had only ever done loving things had been betrayed and deserted by everyone, including all his disciples, which made his final exhibition of love so supreme. This bleak tale also tells us about the Son of Man's courage, forbearance, selflessness, forgiveness, peace and invincible humanity.

The death of Christ was a perfect and complete lesson for man. There was just nothing more to be said. This was God's word. The height and the depth. The truth and the terrible evil that is in us all too. It is all there.

And for what, my people of Wales? For what?

FIERY VALLEYSCAPES

The children have been lighting fires all along the dry walls of the Valleys again and it's a rare day when red and yellow flames are not licking the slopes with huge wraiths of black smoke swirling around the village.

These bouts of arson and vandalism seem to come in waves: one year they are stealing car radios or then they're trying to burn the school down or randomly smashing shop windows or else stealing lead off old chapel roofs.

But now they seem to have come to a collective decision to put the Valley to fire and whole areas of the high walls are mottled with charred and smoking patches which seem to sit well with the burned-out stolen cars which also now lie around the place upside down for month after month. The current number one hit, I'm told, is called Firestarter.

These fires are at their most dramatic at night, of course, with their huge, dancing flames and cracklings that are often amplified by the strange acoustics of the Valley. They have a curious fascination for me, in the way of all fires, and I sometimes fancy that I can see pictures of the Valley's past in them: the Hearts of Oak, the jazz bands, the miners' rallies and those entrancing Harvest Festival services with the wonderful hymns when we all thanked God for the bountiful gifts of the earth.

But I was watching one the other night with small black figures dancing around it, either fighting it or exulting in the flames, and there was a clear and sustained moment when I perceived the whole of the valleyscape as a flickering vision of hell. And as I stood there, rooted in the heart of this vision, the words of God when he spoke to Jeremiah came into my mind: 'The flames are set alight and fed with babies, a thing I never commanded, a thing that never entered my thoughts.'

There is a curious feeling of grief and betrayal in these words and there is no doubt that they also mirror God's current sense of anguish and loss when he looks down on his children dancing around these flaming slopes. *These fires were things that never entered my thoughts.*

There has been a lot of argument about the nature of hell

recently and, as you might expect, the Church of England has come up with a report on it. This report is written in the usual whining, mealy-mouthed style that we have come to expect from the Mother Church – when she is not discussing her vast property portfolio – and concludes that hell is being so opposed to God that you are cast out into an outer darkness of non-being.

Well, those words would go down well with those little arsonists wearing baseball caps the wrong way round, wouldn't they? And what do such words mean anyway? Even Aristotle would have trouble finding meaning in them and it's no wonder the people are leaving the churches and chapels in droves if they have to listen to rubbish like that.

The problem with our churches and chapels seems to be that they are almost never able to see or understand what's in front of their very eyes. There are sound and clear arguments that we are already moving straight into hell and that our own children up there on those slopes are busily breaking our hearts with fires which, along with their crime and other forms of destruction, are becoming a coherent experience of hell for all of us.

We have simply stopped loving them and so now, in the destructive fury that almost always comes with parental neglect, they are trying to put us all to the fire. They are literally going to make all our lives hell on earth. It is all perfect somehow; it's all so completely biblical. You reap what you sow.

So we don't take apples to the chapels to thank God for the harvest anymore and, in consequence, the new harvest is to be seen in charred and smoking fields which yield nothing. The new fruit and crops are fire and smoke. And the ploughmen are our own abandoned children as they come not with ploughs but with matches, hatred and petrol, burning our sacred lands and taking us straight to the hell which, in the hard uncaring of our hearts, we so richly deserve.

SPRING RHAPSODY

Spring is sending great wheels of fermenting sunshine rolling down the walls of the Valley and, on such days, I like to sit bare-footed on a chair in my garden and waggle my old toes with glee.

Everything brightens in the Spring as the sun rises on us all with a singular vivacity and already I am thinking hard about my allotment which is already struggling with weeds I never planted.

Quite a few lambs have been born lately too and I've already spotted some of the mothers taking them down to the dustbins in the village and saying: 'Right, kids, this is where you eat in future.' They'll eat anything at all these sheep – except weeds of course – and the butcher tells me that there's always a big run on lamb chops at this time of year because everyone is hoping to eat the sheep who keeps knocking over their dustbins.

The pink fringes of blossom keep sending fresh wafts of fragrance through the air and I especially like to sit watching the faces of all the daffodils looking up and embracing the sun. The actual flowers turn into golden trumpets of light and you half expect them to break into a little Louis Armstrong number at any moment. There was an old Celtic belief that, on certain days in Spring, the sun actually came out and danced with joy.

The delicate yellow tumbles of the forsythia are normally the first off the starting block in our Spring gardens, closely followed by the tulips whose buds open slowly and shyly before bursting into a sort of brazen hussy splendour.

The river snaking along the Valley floor also takes on an added twinkle with quick brown darts of the trout and the hurrying water making the pebbles keep changing colour from brown to grey and back to brown again. Frogs get into the sewers too and sometimes you can actually hear them all moaning and groaning down there together. Every bird in the Valley seems to be fighting over something or other.

I notice that the young lovers have come out walking arm in arm along the river banks, clearly enjoying those early moments of their young lives when everything seems so serene and wonderful and full of enormous possibilities. Even my old heart still gives a pang when I see two young people enjoying their self-absorbed communion of love.

I have always been attracted to the theory that we can see the life of Christ throughout the seasons and that Spring is the most important season of them all since here we can see and feel and smell the spirit of the resurrection.

This is the time when God affirms his most basic and holy intention to give life back to the dead; a time when he makes all things new again, conjuring up fresh shoots out of the very heart of a dead land. Christ's blood continues surging through the world, it is believed, miraculously feeding and recreating the crops year after year. Each Spring the five thousand are being told that they are going to be fed yet again.

There are many who accuse Caradoc of being a miserable old git, forever droning on in his pulpit about demons and darkness like some Old Testament prophet who has missed the last bus back to the Promised Land, but on Spring days like these Caradoc is a happy old git.

All doubts, fears and darkness are vanquished on such days when the sun is dancing around the sky with joy and the frogs are moaning down in the sewers. God is in his heaven and my Valley becomes the very altar of the world as I sit on my chair in my garden, waggling my bare toes at all the new flowers as my very spirits hang-glide on the fragrant breezes of the great resurrection that awaits believers everywhere.

MIND OF THE FLESH

Mrs Caradoc has been unusually cheerful and affectionate for more than a week now, bringing me tea in bed in the mornings and even whistling a lot as she does her housework and brasses. The reason behind this outbreak of happiness, I have learned, is that someone called Alan finally agreed to marry someone called Carol in *EastEnders*.

Mrs Caradoc has always been a sucker for a good marriage and I remember a lot of whooping and shouting coming out of our front parlour on the night they tied the knot and then there was the usual ritual chin-wag with our neighbour over the garden fence afterwards. Half an hour to watch *EastEnders* and then an hour to discuss it.

This marriage has a special resonance, it seems, since Carol is white and Alan is as black as night. The fervent hope all along the back gardens around here is that this marriage will make it and that the couple will achieve a happiness which has so far evaded them.

Well, for what it's worth, Old Caradoc hopes that Alan and Carol will make it too but, from what he gathers about the antics of the rest of them in *EastEnders*, it is not looking terribly likely since as sure as eggs is eggs one of them is going to start crawling into someone else's bed sooner or later.

I've even heard that there's one motor dealer called, I think, David Wicks, who has about a dozen women on the go. It is simply not humanly possible to get anywhere at all on that basis without damaging and mangling everyone in sight, himself included.

But if Carol and Alan are really as serious about their marriage as pigeons and Roman Catholics, then Old Caradoc has only five words of fine advice: Thou shalt not commit adultery.

There is an awful lot of waffle in the modern media about the breakdown of marriage and and even bigger amount of waffle spoken about love but the real villain of the peace is our growing practice of adultery which is busily wrecking almost every family in sight.

The whole of this wretched Royal family of ours is now in ruins, I suggest, because not one of them obeyed this simple commandment. Not one of the children gave their marriage more than five minutes after it had got into trouble before sneaking off into the arms and beds of another with whom they then developed emotional bonds.

Marriage doesn't just happen with a wave of a bishop's hand; it grows in time and only really begins working when two bodies come to need and depend on one another. It simply can't work in the wonderful way it can; it just doesn't have a chance if one or the other is involved in an adulterous relationship.

Sexual desire, like alcoholism, is never in itself satisfied but there is no finer satisfaction than marital sex whose special joy and release is that, when it's working well, you don't think about it at all, still less go lusting after someone else. Happiness only ever arrives after the first sexual heat has gone.

Every man I've ever met who has divorced now regrets it. No

one I know has ever improved his happiness with a divorce and the abandoned children always, without fail, suffer grievously, learning a pattern of breakdown which they will then probably pass on.

Those who persistently think with what St Paul called the mind of the flesh will only ever experience or cause depression, suicide and pain. A father or mother who abandons their children in these increasingly dangerous days might as well pour acid over them and be done with it. They will never know or feel or deserve happiness in this life again.

So if Alan and Carol really want to make it, all they have to do is keep adultery in the family and keep having an affair with one another. The only requirement is that they cling to the belief in physical faithfulness even when their minds are at odds. Yes, the secret of a good marriage really is as simple as that.

A BEE WARNING

There has been faint turmoil in the Caradoc household all week because a swarm of bees has taken up lodgings in our eaves.

Where these bees came from is a mystery understood by God alone but Mrs Caradoc is not too happy with our new lodgers and neither are several of the busybodies in our terrace who keep dropping by and suggesting that I get them fumigated before they take over the whole village.

Such talk is typical Valleyspeak. Why they always accuse politicians of wild exaggerations I don't know because there are days when I'm sure wild exaggeration was actually invented around here.

But there they all are, standing on my doorstep with their BAs in boloney, and going on and on about how my bees are surely going to attack the local dogs or sting the children or even start ram-raiding the local shop, presumably to try and steal the jars of honey off the shelves rather than go to the bother and trouble of making it themselves.

But the problem here is that Old Caradoc has always been rather fond of bees and several times now he has been forced to deliver a spirited lecture on their behalf, explaining to these dummies that bees are God's creatures with souls of their own and that we shouldn't get the wind up because we saw some daft film about killer bees in the local bughouse when we were kids.

Bees will only ever sting you if you are stupid enough to get in their flight path or reach into their hives and try and molest the queen bee, I tell them. Bees can be extremely nasty and anti-social, it is true, but usually only with one another and often when they've decided that they've had enough of their queen bee, often killing her and simply flinging her body through the front door.

Royalists will doubtless be pleased to learn that complete social anarchy follows this dastardly act with the whole structure of the hive going to pot, workers doing no work, soldiers skiving off when they should have been on guard duty and delinquent gangs of them roaming abroad and roughing up neighbouring hives or else attacking dogs or pensioners.

So all we've got to do, I keep telling everyone, is just to keep checking that there's not the dead body of a queen bee on the pavement outside my front door one morning because, if there is, that's a sure sign that the mucky stuff is about to hit the fan.

Now there are three or four of my neighbours minutely examining the pavement outside my house every morning even if the bees seem to be getting along with one another fine, being obedient to their queen and flying in and out of their front door like the energetic and sturdy fighter pilots they all are.

It was St Cuthbert, of course, who once developed a marvellous relationship with birds in general and his ducks in particular. He even used to like standing in the cold sea all night in prayer when a few seals would pop out in the morning and dry him off.

St Francis also had a wonderful and intuitive understanding of all animals; they were brothers and sisters to him and he even called them by name, Brother Ass, Brother Wolf, and so on.

So, in the spirit of these great spiritual ancestors of ours, Old Caradoc is now trying to develop a love relationship with the bees in his roof, even if, just yet, he can't quite work out which is which and give them their own names since they all look pretty much the same.

But before we go any further perhaps it had better be publicly recorded right now that they've only got to bump off their queen once or sting Mrs Caradoc once or get the dog next door once and this love relationship is going to be called off immediately. Furthermore, any sign of anarchy in the rafters and the whole lot of them are going to be evicted with the aid of a fumigation gun or something equally unpleasant without any further notice. So be warned, boys. Be warned.

CELEBRATIONS OF EVIL

All of us hope to pass on something to our children or the world, no matter how small, but I wonder if anyone has ever managed to bequeath a legacy quite as diseased and squalid as Dennis Potter's *Karaoke*?

This truly repulsive television series, penned in the playwright's final days, is not so much a final bequest to the world as an expensive and spectacular act of revenge on a world which he clearly hated. It might also serve as a masterful, new definition of how far and how low the modern artist has sunk.

Karaoke's major sin is that nothing in it resonates with reality and, rather than being shown any aspects of the real world or real people, we are merely taken on a grand tour of the seedy crevices of Potter's self-indulgent imagination.

There is a persistent refusal to distinguish between dream and reality and this is, from first to last, the work of a dirty and dying old man with masturbatory fantasies of young flesh. This is the self-absorbed drivel of an artistic mind which, in its final days, failed to make any connections with anything other than his empty sexual yearnings.

The non-ideas are told in a non-language spattered with four-lettered words and studded with glimpses of perverted sex such as the woman who, for some inexplicable reason, was being assaulted anally and violently again and again.

All the characters are depraved or twisted in some way. Sensation is repeatedly cultivated for its own sake and the plot meanders continually through its own incoherent meaningless-ness. Every scene seems to contain some act or threat of violence.

But a further legacy of this major artistic disaster is that, in a fortnight when we also saw the repulsive *Alien* on our screens and we also witnessed a detailed act of sexual congress on a lavatory floor in *Captives* and the hateful *Kids* was released in our cinemas, the doors of decency were well and truly kicked in again.

In a fortnight in which we have also seen that naked and gaudy celebration of evil that is the Cannes Film Festival Potter has managed to set up a new benchmark in destructive depravity. This mob of modern artists has yet again found a new standard bearer and their vicious assault on the world and all our children continues unabated.

It will all get a good deal worse yet and the chatter of bullets in Dunblane and Tasmania are but the early cuckoos of a long, hot season in hell which is daily going to propel us all into an ever-deepening nightmare.

The romantic mind of the modern artist, which loves violence in all its forms, was clearly behind these terrible crimes – as it is behind most of the others which are now threatening us all. Our screens and the people who run them are busy seeping evil into every corner of our lives as even Dustin Hoffman seems to have worked out for himself.

Immoral in its ethics, barbarous in its aesthetics and destitute of anything that might pass for rational thought, this romantic mind has attacked the very mind, heart and ideas of God.

This mind, which sits squarely at the centre of the mystery of modern lawlessness, has become both the product and cause of the decline of Christianity. In its murderous excesses it far outstrips even the wildest dreams of Hitler and all his Nazis. It represents, quite simply, the biggest wave of evil that the world has yet seen.

Old Caradoc, in his battered Welsh pulpit, reminds the people of Wales that, through their television licences, they are funding the evil of Potter's mob, with all their lies and their persistent fantasies of depravity and violence.

He wants to know what happened to the Welsh conscience. He demands that the Welsh stop lying on their backs like stricken, spineless dogs. He is here and now telling them to get up and show their teeth and start growling their defiance by throwing their boot at the TV.

GLITTERING VISIONS

I enjoyed a wonderful and warm moment with God the other afternoon as I sat on a rock on the banks of the River Wye just above Tintern letting the cold water swirl around the bunions of my old feet.

Rivers have the widest range of moods but that afternoon the pool-and-riffle curves of the Wye, stirred up by days of rain, were sprinting along past old mills and beneath even older iron bridges, with all the obsessed determination of a track racer.

These waters had probably sprung up just as fast in the very bowels of the Cambrian Mountains and were now rushing for an urgent appointment with the great tidal rips of the Severn Estuary. Occasionally you can see a salmon leap out this way but all I could spot in the deep pools were the darting movements of sticklebacks or eels or even perhaps a rainbow trout. A few ducks went past too and there were the question mark necks of a couple of swans.

William Wordsworth wrote about the river's 'soft inland murmur' but it is always something of a marvel to me that you can rarely hear anything of the river's natural music at all, particularly given its size and speed. The odd trickle, yes, but mostly a graveyard silence.

But it was while glorying in the constant movement of light on water that I had one of my moments of pilgrim epiphany, seeing the bars of shadow and sunlight piling up together until it was almost as if the whole clear luminous hand of God was stretching out over the glittering water.

Then, directly beneath the palm of this huge and holy hand, I spotted the V-shape of a hunting otter, turning this way and that, looking for fish. At that moment the whole scene reduced me to tears and I wanted to call out to the otter and invite him home for a cup of tea or something. But I was weeping so much I couldn't cry out any words at all.

The Wye has never had the industry which polluted rivers like the Taff, killing off the fish and animal life, but it was still thrilling seeing this rare and wonderful animal up and doing in this clear, pure water.

Members of the old Celtic Church actually worshipped at wells of clear water. They believed in the purity of water long before our modern Greens got hold of the idea but, there again, the Greens filched just about all their ideas from the old Celtic Church.

There was the cry of a child from somewhere in the distant woods on the opposite bank and this giant hand of light began changing shape again, turning into a large yet formless shadow before sinking down and disappearing into the hurrying river.

It has taken Old Caradoc a long time to discern the holiness and meaning of this moment; this shifting, airy tableau on the Wye which, on reflection, seemed to contain so much about life and God's most basic promise that everything, in time, will be refashioned and renewed with his very own hand.

We should think of God as the carpenter of all life except that he does not work with wood, like his son in his Nazarene youth, but with fire and light and water. Water, as both the bringer and giver of all life, has always been his most basic raw material. It is the means of baptism, faith and cure. It is the natural habitat of every hunting otter and fish and God knows exactly where all of them are at any one moment, even those lurking at the bottom of the deepest and darkest ocean.

Water is also our most basic raw material. We were all conceived in the waters of the womb; it almost wholly sustains our bodies throughout our long lives and it is to the very waters of the earth that we will all one day return.

STRANGER IN A STORM

The sunshine has been busy blow-torching the Valley slopes almost all June now, often burning every rock and tree and making lots of white butterflies keep tumbling about in the shimmering heat hazes.

Our allotments are doing well nevertheless but, no matter how much we water the plants, there is no substitute for real rain and there are hours when you can almost actually hear the parched and cracked earth crying out for relief.

A rescue of sorts came the other day when, almost without warning, there was a brief and spectacular build-up of black cloud at the top of the Valley accompanied by a loud crack of thunder. Lightning stabbed through the very heart of the black cloud and you could see the whole unruly gang of them marching down on us like a war party of Vikings intent on a bout of pillaging and rape.

The others left but I stayed in my allotment shed and left the door open as I lit my pipe and sat on a box watching this storm rage all around. There are all the deep and furious elements of God in a storm and I know exactly why the painter JMW Turner liked to be strapped to a ship's mast in a storm so that he could better understand and paint it.

Rain hammered on the shed roof and hissed into the water butts as yet more lightning kept slicing through the summer thunder. Water leaked through my roof too, vibrating the cobwebs around my old plant pots and the legs of the spiders appeared briefly to see what they had caught.

This storm didn't seem to want to pass over either and, within an hour or so, night had fallen as the Valley slopes continued to be shaken by the thunder and washed by torrents of rain.

I remained staring out into the storming darkness with a calm imperturbability when lightning illuminated every corner of the Valley and I noticed a dark and unfamiliar figure walking down past my potato rows towards me in a shivering revelation. He seemed to have crept straight out of the interstices of the storm.

He had large eyes with a beard and a white shirt which seemed to be curiously dry in all this rain. His feet were sandalled and the stammering lightning made his walk jerky, almost unreal, and I bit my lip, feeling strangely confused.

I half-expected that this stranger might be coming to my shed to take shelter but he disappeared into the rainy darkness and, with the next revelation of lightning, it was clear that he had gone missing altogether.

I went out into the allotment to take a closer look around with my torch but there was nothing and no one anywhere except the rain shaking the leaves of the young potato plants. Neither could I find any trace of his sandal prints in the muddy old path. The rain washed over my face and hair as I wiped my eyes uselessly with my fingertips.

My earlier imperturbability had also gone so I returned to my shed and crashed to my knees where I put down my torch and sniffed a lot as my heart seemed to be pounding about as loudly as the surrounding storm.

A spider actually made me jump as it wandered slowly and delicately through the yellow splash of light left by my torch on the shed floor rather like some shy, leggy ballerina wandering into the spotlight to accept some tumultuous applause.

And it was there on my knees watching the spider take its curtain call that I recalled that The Second Coming is referred to 318 times in the 210 chapters of the New Testament. It is the Son of Man's most repeated promise. 'When I return to you,' he kept saying. 'I will not leave you as orphans.'

When he walks back onto the stage of the world it will be as sudden as it is unexpected. This day will come like a thief in the night. The dead in Christ will rise and he will come as lightning. He will come with a shout, with the voice of an archangel, with the very trump of God.

So how long now, oh Lord? How long?

Alcoholic wreckage

We buried Marie Jones–Walters last Tuesday in the village and, while all funerals are never particularly joyful, this one was especially tough to take because Marie was only 53.

They found her in the gutter just outside the Welfare Hall at around four in the morning. It had been raining hard, they said, and she looked like some strange rag doll as she lay face down with all the rain washing all around her body.

What was even worse than that was that she must have been lying there for around five hours and there would have been many in the Hall who would have walked straight past her. I'm not saying that they deliberately ignored her – we haven't got quite that bad yet – but I am saying that they were all probably too drunk to see anything with any clarity. Rather like Marie.

I knew Marie all her life and remember well those days when she was in school and would come around here to run errands for Mrs Caradoc. She was a bright, vivacious girl with a sixpenny gap in her teeth and always much sought after by the boys.

She was bright enough to have gone to Oxford and I used to loan her some of my books, hoping that she might even develop a taste for theology, but she didn't because she fell in love with a boy in the next terrace and they married.

This boy left her for another woman and broke Marie's heart. She took to bingeing heavily on weekends and, in the collapse of the critical faculties that always comes with heavy drinking, she often ended up in bed with some truly horrible men. She hated herself for this and drank even more.

She lost her job in Cardiff, had her home re-possessed and went back to live with her Aunty. The drinking got worse and she was sent to dry out several times but with no success. The pain was unbelievable and she came to see me a few times, telling me about it.

One afternoon she lay concealed in a flower bed near the bowling green, listening to everyone walking past and wondering why she couldn't be normal like them. She was hiding in her room a lot too, actually sitting on a cushion on top of her bottle in case anyone called – except, of course, no one ever did.

The wonder boys in the social services decided that there was no point in trying to dry her out any further and even gave her an allowance for alcohol. She soon became a pitiful and wretched figure around the village, losing her looks and a lot of her hair, often stopping people in the terraces and asking them to catch her because she was about to fall over. They often never quite knew what to do and then she just fell over.

So she finally fell over for the last time and died in that rainy gutter outside the Welfare Hall, yet another killed by drink; yet another drunken statistic. Hers was a visible even dramatic death but there are untold thousands of others who are now, in many subtle and devious ways, dying exactly like poor Marie.

Drink is a great modern evil; it is a poison which is far more potent, destructive and widespread than any of the youngsters' drugs. Alcoholism is the disease that always insists that it's not there; it is a self-imposed prison from which there is rarely any escape. Alcohol is the one drug that makes you feel better while it kills you at the same time; the only word it truly understands is *more*. One drink is always enough, two is too many and three is not nearly enough.

It has been killing all the Valley tribes for years now and is becoming daily ever more adept at killing our children, our families, our careers, our health and our very relationship with God. Nothing is ever beyond its predatory reach as it takes every person and reduces them to just the rags on their back.

Then, soon, rather like Marie Jones-Walters, it will reach out and even take them.

SPIRITUALIZED BODIES

Our gorgeous Indian summer has long gone with cold drizzle frequently streaming down the brown and gold sides of the Valley.

Sometimes the sun will make a guest appearance but mostly it is one long story of mists chasing and curling around one another, often settling on the rooftops of the terraces like an army of ghosts taking a long rest after a particularly energetic mass haunting.

These are not good days for anyone in the Valleys. Even the dimmest now accept that everything has gone woefully wrong and await the coming night with growing fear. Cars are being broken into routinely, homes burgled and drugs injected. There was a particularly murderous fight outside the Welfare Hall the other night and a few had to be taken to hospital.

With everything in such a lost and fallen state Old Caradoc walks and broods and looks. Generally all he sees are yet more signs of our destructive sin and faithlessness although, a few days ago, there was a new twist in the plot.

The autumnal mists were particularly thick one afternoon when I was passing the old cemetery and my ears were arrested by a form of music. Oh aye, the druggies have moved in there now with their ghetto-blasters, I thought, but, as I moved closer, I saw a number of silvery figures standing among the headstones, all of them motionless and staring directly ahead of them.

It was most extraordinary as I moved among these people all standing there as quietly and calmly as if they were waiting for a bus. A motionless woman was holding the hand of a motionless child. An old miner was there with his hands on his hips. Here a hunched pensioner. There a youngster in a baseball cap on the other way around, recently buried I believe.

The sound of weeping rose into the air as I walked down the main path between the tombstones and spoke to them but they made no reply before disappearing abruptly like ghosts at dawn. That strange music came back for a while but that died away too.

I've been thinking a lot about my vision of these mysterious and static souls in the cemetery and decided they had come together to say something about the nature of their grief and demonstrate the power of the resurrection. Thy dead shall live, their bodies shall rise, the Bible says. O dwellers in the dust awake.

The Bible also promised that our physical bodies would be transmuted into spiritualized bodies and surely that's what had happened here. The spiritualized bodies of my people had returned to the place of their earthly burial to pay witness. But to what exactly?

A witness to the death of their own people? A witness to the way their descendants had come to defile the perfect body of creation? A witness to the way we have dishonoured that for which they had once lived? That weeping suggested a deep and intractable sorrow.

Yet St Paul told us that Christ is the first fruit of those that sleep. He is the first-begotten from the dead and death shall finally be overcome. So could these figures be telling me something about new moves by Christ in his world? Or could they have been there about to make a Pentecostal warning about some sudden new move of the Holy Spirit? Or were they there, as I had first suspected, merely to wring their hands in weeping postures of lament?

I don't know. There was a lot that was missing and a lot more that made no sense at all. But I will be keeping a weather eye on that cemetery in the future in the hope and prayer that it may yet reveal more clues to the enigma that is the resurrection. I also very much want to hear what those who sleep in the dust of the earth might be trying to tell those of us who are dead but also alive in these dark and doomed times of autumnal Valley mists.

Our Childhood Mecca

Moslems are expected to go to Mecca at least once in their lives; Roman Catholics often opt for Rome or Lourdes and we of the battered collier tribe of South Wales always made an annual pilgrimage to Barry Island.

The Whitsun treat train ride to Barry Island, complete with a tanner, a new pair of daps and a pair of knitted bathers, which often shrank to a fig leaf on contact with cold, brown water, almost amounted to a penitential rite.

Long-forgotten faces always turned up in chapel a week or two before the Whitsun treat – to qualify for the big trip – and then we all packed on trains to get to this potty little seaside resort when we would invariably be greeted by a strong downpour of rain.

'Barry Island has been the jewelled eye in the childhood summers of millions of us,' wrote Gwyn Thomas. 'At the first sight and sound of us the fish moved off a mile and kept a cold eye on the whole Sunday School movement that had sponsored our act of joy. Once a year, one magic glimpse of the sea.'

I went back to this place of all my childhood pilgrimages again last week and found Barry locked in some strange identity crisis and undergoing odd changes, not all of them to the good. Every shop in the town itself was newly shuttered, almost as if they had all been ram-raided the night before. A man told me that the police had got a set of new mountain bikes to chase burglars into the outlying estates but, on the night of the bikes' delivery, the whole lot had been stolen.

Some clown had also put washing powder into the fountain in front of the Town Hall on the day I was there with predictably silly results.

But the island itself seems to have been given a lively facelift with lots of new cobbling along the old prom and I also enjoyed the fat, lovely sounds of a brass band ooompah-oompahing through some old favourites. I really do hope they have brass bands in heaven.

The fairground itself has also been totally transformed with even some decent new lavatories which are in themselves a big advance on the old days. The high mountain walls of the old scenic railway, which re-arranged the shape of your face for a good week, have also gone, as have many of the seedier stalls where you could buy candy floss which locked your teeth together, or you could spend a fortune trying to win a goldfish with a life expectancy of about three minutes.

I also like the cheapness and quiet vulgarity of the wares in the new Hypervalue shop in the fairground; a shop which in many ways reminds me of the old Woolworths chain of stores before they got airs and graces. Hypervalue is in the fine traditions of the old Valley shops.

The smell of chips remains the same as does the call of the gulls and the lazy roars of the sea.

Another relative newcomer to Barry of course is that huge holiday camp on the next headland which seems both so enticing and yet forbidding that I have never dared set foot in there, possibly in case I never got out again. I sometimes catch myself looking up at it with my mind boggling at what goes on in there. It could be almost anything at all.

But the one part of Barry which never changes, of course, is the marvellous sweep of its great sands and, even with the winds ripping all around me, I stood out there for maybe an hour listening again to all the laughter and uproar and pure, untrammelled happiness of my chapel youth.

For the day – and just for the day – we were all connected in a gentling sense of love. I don't suppose that I have ever been as happy or as complete or as full of hope as I was in those gilded days when, wearing my new daps and with a tanner in my pocket, I made my childhood pilgrimage to Barry.

Here, on these sands, we were as all children should be; having fun beneath the benevolent gaze of a loving God who was also having fun as he watched us play and everything was just fine, both in heaven and on earth.

THE MENACE OF MONEY

The peculiar failure of the modern pulpit, it has long seemed to me, is that it has somehow become perceived as a bastion of interference and oppression when nothing could be less likely

The pulpit in Wales both encouraged and inspired the people while also trying to help them live more abundantly. The most basic ambition of the Welsh pulpit was not to enslave the flock with restrictions but to offer them visions and insights which would set them free.

Sexual promiscuity, for example, forever masquerades as a freedom but is nothing less than a heavy shackle with devastating and destructive consequences for all who come near or indulge in it. Alcohol is also often presented as a key to freedom and happiness but that too can lead to a self-imposed prison from which, for some, there will never be any escape. The role of the pulpit has always been to attack and expose such illusions again and again.

But what now is a greater yoke on all of us than this National Lottery which, each week, I am growing to detest more and more if only because it is the poor who are largely funding it?

This Lottery has come to enshrine all the principles of modern Mammon and is now perhaps the prime example of how this evil Thatcherite culture of ours is busy eating into the balance and well-being of almost every home and personality.

Mammon, encouraged to an unprecedented degree by that Thatcher woman, is now attacking everyone and everything, actively destroying our once proud institutions like banks who these days – and almost without exception – are not much more principled than the average barrow boy.

Our Members of Parliament couldn't be any more venal either since they have yet again spat squarely on the poor, the weak and the unemployed by voting themselves a 33 per cent wage rise. Despite their persistent squawking about poverty when did you last read of an MP starving to death?

Jesus was the most insightful and radical critic of money who ever lived. He spoke of money more times than any other subject except the Kingdom of God. You cannot worship God and Mammon, he kept saying. Woe to the rich. Blessed are the poor. Give until you bleed.

He understood clearly that money was a dark and implacable power, demonic and destructive by nature. Again and again he taught that for many it had become a god which demanded to be worshipped in its own right.

This god would seek control of our minds and hearts and then keep us enslaved because the urge to acquire money, like nymphomania, would never, ever be satisfied. We all know of the wealthy who spend every waking hour trying to become more wealthy and never think of giving so much as a penny to the poor.

When Jesus cleansed the Temple, in his only known act of violence, he was saying, symbolically, how the land had to be first cleansed of Mammon. But, today, Mammon reigns supreme and every political attempt to break his power has failed.

So what you see when you see a queue of people for Lottery tickets is a queue of greedy, Thatcherite fools waiting to throw away their money at the feet of Mammon. You are seeing one of the last rites of a lost, empty-headed tribe who have abandoned all spirituality and become dumb and unhappy slaves as they kneel in a shrine dedicated to laying waste the world and keeping the poor ever poorer.

Also remember that, if you buy a ticket on Monday, you have statistically a better chance of being knocked over and killed on the road, than you have of collecting the jackpot the following Saturday. And the irony is that, if you do win the Jackpot, you are then the real loser. These are the golden rules of Mammon, my friends, and they never, ever change.

Arise and tear up your Lottery tickets, oh people of Wales. You have nothing to lose but your chains.

A COMPLEX GOD

This pulpit has told you again and again of the unremitting and endless heartbreak of God; of the way that he fears for the future of his children and of his mounting anxiety about the way tides of evil are flooding every home.

Ah, so what, it seems to be the response of many who no longer seem to believe in him anyway. Poor old God. Perhaps we'd all have been better off if he hadn't made the world in the first place. Perhaps he'd be best advised to go off and work on another more fruitful project.

One of the main problems of our faithless age is that no one seems to have any clear picture of God. Many of the old still persist in thinking of him as a bearded and benign old duffer sitting on a throne in the clouds while many of our dim-witted theologians are forever trying to peddle us some odd and fanciful concept that he is merely love, whatever that means, or depth or something vague inside us which can mean whatever we want it to mean.

But, even on a cursory reading of the Old Testament, we find that God is a tremendous, riven personality who is both a destroyer and creator, the one side of his complex character constantly battling with the other. We encounter a God given to volcanic bouts of anger who can also get rampantly murderous, flooding the world, levelling Sodom, destroying the enemies of Israel and then, touchingly, often regretting it. He is anarchic and riotously unpredictable. Sometimes he does not seem to know his own mind and appears a mystery even to himself.

We also learn of a God who is often neither male nor female and, on occasion, appears androgynous. When he made the world he had no past, no private or sex life, no wife and no one to befriend. He does not think like us and no one has ever seen his face. When Moses asked him who he was and what he was up to he merely replied, with fantastic self-confidence: 'I am what I am.' End of explanation.

At heart he often appears as a pure and exultant warrior, raining boils, fire and brimstone on his enemies, conquering Egypt and destroying the Caananites but, when his troops give up on him, he gives up on them. He can also be awesomely truculent, once turning a woman into a block of salt. This is a brooding, jealous God who simply will not tolerate the worship of other gods. For long periods he will go quiet and then explode into an awesome rage.

But then he can become a most solicitous father, a personal friend to the friendless, demanding our love and fear. His moods are often exceptionally tender while he can also be a personal advocate and lawgiver.

The strangest of the strange, the Lord God also appointed some even stranger men to be his prophets. With their wild veerings and ravaged visions they all had a questionable sanity. His prophets were almost all psychotics or depressives while one of them lived with a prostitute and another in a cave. They were all also reluctant to get into prophecy and had to be dragooned into it.

This God of ours is also clearly an insomniac who demands our praise right around the clock. His finest and best qualities were reflected in his only son but there is also a lot that is dark and questionable about his multiple contradictions. History, in a sense, is the story of our God trying to work out his own inner contradictions in relationship to his people with whom he also constantly suffers. As we bleed then so does he. Without us he is as nothing.

So this is something of the size and colour and shape of the divine personality which holds us all in the hollow of his hand. This is the father destined to be our father forever; the one and only Lord, red in tooth and claw, creator and destroyer, shepherd and nagging wife, cruel bully and loving angel, who is now working out his life in relationship to a people who have broken the covenant he once imposed upon them.

This also is the Lord God who really is not going to sit back for too much longer, withdrawn and heartbroken, as he watches his children being destroyed in much the same and certain way as they destroyed his only son.

ᚒPPIES AND DOWNIES

Once upon a time there was a fine old Celtic kingdom called the Land Beyond the Waves, a place of beauty and abundance. There were two main tribes in this Land Beyond the Waves who, although sharing much the same religion with the same personal saviour, occasionally broke into prolonged bickering over whether soccer penalties should be kicked into the top of the net or into the bottom corner. They were called the Uppies and Downies.

This bickering lasted for years and even decades when, lo, an old Celtic demon returned to the land after being banished many centuries ago by the patron saint of the Land Beyond the Waves. This demon was called Corna and his sole pleasure was to cause trouble and strife wherever possible.

Corna was a great master of illusion and entertainment with such a glittering and attractive personality that he was able to present himself as a friend and educator of the people, often declaring himself a champion of both tribes and seemingly able to make both the Uppies and Downies laugh or cry at will.

Neither of the two main tribes could see or understand the pure evil in Corna's heart and they even put up an image to him in every home and on every hearth.

But then Corna began his work with such a brazen and magical power that no one at all could see what was happening. He would sit in silence for a long time looking around the Land Beyond the Waves and waiting for some trouble. And when it did start he would seize on it and, using his formidable magic powers, he would send exaggerated reports of it into every home.

And, lo, all the Uppies and Downies became confused and frightened by this violent imagery and blamed one another. A few more acts of violence broke out as result of Corna's reports and again Corna caught hold of these small violent acts and pumped them back into every home. Then more violence broke out and he busily kept recycling it until it seemed that the whole of the Land had collapsed into anarchy and war.

But also, unfortunately, in both tribes, was a tiny gang of lunatics who, rather than shooting the ball into the bottom or top of the net, actually favoured blowing the ball up with a swift explosion. These lunatics – the Boomers – were despised by most of the Uppies and Downies but were mightily loved by Corna since he adored the purity and intensity of their violence. He loved their lack of pretension or any coherent arguments, promoting them totally out of proportion to their importance. The Boomers were always sensationally visual.

Yet, even so, the main tribes still continued to blame one

another and the work of Corna was so masterful and well dis-
guised that almost no one blamed him for anything at all with
even the church leaders and representatives of both tribes always
anxious to curry his favour. The few who did try and finger
Corna were immediately left talking to themselves since this
brilliant demon had all but taken over almost all the lines of
communication. 'I am trying to help you all out,' he told the few
ingrates who did try and challenge him. 'All I'm doing is trying
to explain to everyone what's going on. I have nothing to do
with any of this violence. Nothing.'

Soon the Uppies were fighting with the Downies again until
the very streets were running with blood and, even when a
temporary truce was called, Corna soon found a way of subvert-
ing it, since all he needed to do was focus on one small act of
violence – just one Boomer nutcase! – and he managed to get
the whole pot stirred up and boiling again.

And thus Corna, unopposed and unchallenged, managed to
keep rivers of violence and fire running through the Land
Beyond the Waves for year after year. His persistent distortions
and lies broke every attempt at peace. As the old prophet Isaiah
had it, the truth had stumbled in the streets and honesty could not
enter. It finally came to pass that the land became a smoking ruin
and the few Uppies and Downies left alive couldn't even recall
what their traditional tribal row had been over in the first place.

A RIVER BAPTISM

Rivers have always called out to me in much the same way as
pubs appear to call out to alcoholics and it is all but impossible
for me to pass a river without actually stopping to glory in it
from the bank.

The river Taff is looking particularly gorgeous this summer,
bowling down through the old coalfields, sparkling with dazzling
drifts of light and coming on so fresh and clean that she might
have sprung up from those distant, purple mountains only last
week.

The Taff was black and dead for all my life, thick with coal-dust and belly-up fish, where even the eels had trouble staying alive, until the Tories put the final boot into the mines, which closed down the coal washeries and gave this river another chance. 'Tis an ill wind . . .

Now otters have returned to secret places along the river and there are often iridescent flashes of hunting kingfishers or even salmon leaping the weirs. Mullet feed openly in the waving weeds.

When possible, I always like to say my morning prayers on a river bank and I was preparing to do just that the other morning on the Taff when I spotted an act so perfect that it sent my spirits hang-gliding on the river breezes.

At first I thought that it was just two fishermen moving about in the silvery water when I saw that one man was, in fact, baptizing the other. They were there for about ten minutes performing this simple and tender act of communion right there on this fantastic altar of a great river.

And as I watched them, sending them the support of my prayers, my mind ranged back to another river that I once visited years ago, the Jordan, in whose muddy waters, for reasons too complicated to explain fully here, I was also once baptized by an eight-foot tall Negro from Macon Rouge.

I had been visiting the Yardenit Pilgrimage Centre with a chapel group and this Negro pastor the height of a skyscraper dunked the lot of us, with full honours and glorious gospel songs. Afterwards and still dripping wet, I preached to all of them about the meaning of baptism.

John the Baptist was the first herald of the coming of Christ, I told them. We know that he was a tremendous, riven man, burly and bearded, who dressed in camel skins and fed on a diet of locusts and wild honey. Shield your eyes and see him now, wandering out of those brown and barren hills of Judea. Listen hard and you will still hear that massive voice crying in the wilderness.

When John baptized Jesus just here it was the first time a human had become involved in the public ministry of the Son of Man. Right here the veil between heaven and earth was finally stripped away and, in those muddy waters, a battle was enjoined which is still being fought to this day. They flung John into prison and he was beheaded at Salome's request but we can still see him rising in his cell and pounding those walls right to the end with his angry fists. When the truth is imprisoned within you it always demands to be free. He would have known that the people killed all God's prophets but defiance would always have been his.

And so it was that, with these words and memories stirring in my mind, I watched that man being baptized in the fresh waters of the River Taff the other morning. Out of new water another new man was rising. Death is always a prelude to more life.

This is also the time of St John's Tide; a midsummer festival which is both a celebration of light, life and the great man himself. The Baptist's is the awesome shadow in which we could all still find some shade. We could all be revived again by the courage he showed when everyone spat on him. Through him we could find the defiant words to cry out against the destructive tides of lawlessness in which we are all drowning.

The Baptist is the man through whom we can come to understand the mystery of faith. His life reminds us of our duty to be the devoted children of a God who will never be driven from his throne. 'Prepare the way of the Lord. Make his path straight. The day of the Messiah is at hand.'

OUR SACRED NATION

Your nation is like your faith; it abides deep in the heart of you, as enduring and yet invisible as fervent prayer. This nation is your present and past, welded together by memory and experience, moulded by ancestral voices and unified by the quiet terror that comes with a deep and holy walk with God.

Our nation is beyond opposition or insult if only because outsiders can never really know what is in our hearts; they will never quite know what it is that keeps giving us quickening bursts of pride through our every vein.

They will never know this because we don't really know ourselves; we all, each one of us, build our own unique picture of our nationhood from a wide complexity of often unlikely detail.

When Old Caradoc thinks of Wales he pictures lonely stone chapels and preachers quietly exhorting a small congregation with words of inspiration and love; he feels a sense of kindly decency in the terraces; he hears a great burst of excitement as Cliff Morgan runs through the opposing backs and always, without fail, he smells and even tastes tea brewing on the kitchen range.

But deep within all this tribal detail is the backbone of our enduring values. These will be the values of fellowship and hospitality to strangers; of scholarship and instinct for democracy; of the ability to take a moral stand despite appalling opposition and our historic desire to give praise to God.

Our nation's relationship with God stretches back to St David and beyond. It has been a long and often passionate relationship which still lives in our rugby grounds on the day of the international. It might well have worn a bit thin in our churches and chapels, of course, but Wales has had more revivals than any other land in the world. The offer of God's love is always on the table; it is always there waiting to be picked up.

Yet we seem to be losing sight of all this, I am sensing, and often with some reason when we survey our current plagues of Lottery-mania, drug addiction, youth crime and the money-grabbing antics of these wretched rugby players of ours.

We seem to be getting wounded and low and listening to the distant insults of empty hacks who take an immature and idiotic delight in telling us we are worthless and then watching our hackles rise. In our secret thoughts we begin wondering if perhaps it really is true. We are asking ourselves if we are going to win anything ever again. Oh for a great athlete or even a decent soccer team. Just one good darts player would be something, oh Lord. Just one!

It really is time for all this nonsense to stop. We have simply got to start feeling good about ourselves again. We must lift ourselves up off our knees and stand at full height with shoulders thrown back.

Yet we are simply not going to achieve that by droning on about how we've got Tom Jones or Shirley Bassey or Anthony Hopkins or the Welsh language or even, God help us all, Dylan Thomas.

What we must do is recall all these things that I have been

telling you about our sacred nationhood. We must reach into our past and remember that this past is also our present and our future. Oh yes, our concept of nationhood may well get wounded or exhausted at times but our nation will ultimately endure for as long as the mountain range of Snowdonia.

This nation will endure and triumph because she is the holding arch of the great Welsh adventure of the mind. She will always be here because there will always be a goodness and kindness in her heart which will live forever. No matter how lost or fallen she may appear to be, Wales will always hold aloft timeless values and beautiful ideals beneath which everyone – even the Welsh – will always be welcome to take shelter.

INDIAN SUMMER OF GLORY

It is always heartening to see that most gracious and lovely of the seasons unfolding around our heads particularly as the autumn reflects my own stage of life too.

When I see the leaves turning brown and falling I see myself and my failing body. When I see the last of the summer wasps flying around, without much puff and barely the aggression to sting anything at all, I sense my own fading strength.

On some rich autumnal days I catch sight of my very soul rolling around the brown bracken slopes of the Valley in convulsive spasms of joy and I even catch reflections of my being in my dying tomato plants, with the leaves curling and drooping as the tomatoes just hang there, fat and red, offering the one last gift of their ripe fruit. You have had my life, now help yourself to its fruit.

All these mellow feelings are also underpinned by the last of our Indian summer days. Enjoy the warmth of my kiss for a few more hours yet since, soon now, everything is going to turn into cold and squalling rain. Enjoy me while you can; say yes to my, briefly, proffered lips because they are not going to be proffered for too much longer. Oh aye, the autumn is my season all right.

But this is not the fugue of an old and dying man, leaning on the lectern of an oak pulpit and glorying vaguely in our autumnal

hues so much as someone trying to compose a hymn of acceptance to what has been a long Valley life. This is the hymn of an
old man who is completely at peace with himself; a man who
has neither side of him at war with the other.

And here in the autumn of his years Old Caradoc came to
this peace when he said yes both to the word of God and all the
comfortable and uncomfortable corners of his own life. He
finally came to this peace when he accepted that God did indeed
hold the world in the palm of his hand and the reason why he
allowed such as war, starvation and crime was a reason known
only to himself which will be fully and finally disclosed in time.
These are not conclusions of hope but of faith.

But not only do we not generally accept the word of God,
we don't even believe in him. We have become disillusioned,
angry and drunken nihilists; we leave our wives in search of
better sex, we abandon our children with callous selfishness for
some mirage of happiness on some distant desert and we give
up on everything there is and turn to the bottle because events
have not turned out the way we planned them. We wanted
everything the other way around; we simply could not accept
things the way they are.

And so we find ourselves choking on the bitter pills of
unhappiness and despair; we have all become the lost children
in a dark and evil wood because we could not bring ourselves
to say yes to our lives, to our partners and our children and
the bills that remained unpaid and the neighbours who play the
piano in the middle of the night and the sheep who keep
knocking over our dustbins and all the other discords that add
up to life on a Welsh earth.

We kept rebelling, wanting it to be different and convinced
that it might even be different if we could somehow engineer
ourselves somewhere else in a new home with a new partner
and new children only to find that, horror of horrors, here too
the neighbours play the piano in the middle of the night in the
same way and the sheep keep knocking over our dustbins in the
same way and the bills keep arriving in the same way and even
these new children keep crying and snivelling in the same way.

We kept saying no when all our lives would become touched
with a new Indian summer of happiness if we had only started

saying yes. All our lives would receive a new kiss of new life if we merely let go of the past and started saying yes; if we merely accepted our life instead of constantly fighting to re-shape it and somehow make it better. And all this is one of the secrets of an autumnal faith: the simple ability to say yes.

BUTTERFLIES OF FAITH

We know that the sun will come up in the morning as surely as it will go down again at night. We know a drink or pill will make us feel better for a few hours and it is far preferable to make ten pounds than five. We know the Lottery is drawn on Saturday night and there is something seriously amiss with Mystic Meg. These are all self-evident visible facts in which we have faith.

But what we have lost, almost without trace, is faith in invisible facts. We believe only in what we can see – or hope to profit or get drunk by – and, with this one philosophic mistake, have propelled ourselves into a lost and confusing world in which we have become lost and confused too.

Faith is way of living by truth or trust in the invisible nature of God's grace; it is to pin our hopes on the ideals of a Saviour to help us through the long, dark night; it is to send up one long call on God to gather us up in his arms and protect us from our enemies.

Within this faith we are then equipped to deal with the multiple and growing horrors of the modern world; within this chrysalis of belief we can transform ourselves into splendid butterflies who can flutter over our spreading waste lands, aloof from death and decay as we revel in our astonishing and defiant beauty.

But, far more than an essential armour, this faith then becomes the private garden in which our love and human kindliness grow; this faith gives us a meaning within which we are both able to maintain our mental well-being and live with, if not actually fight, all the threatening evils of this modern world.

Indeed, it is only through faith that the modern world makes any sense. The faithless man has every right and expectation to see one monumental disaster all around him which is, every day and in every way, becoming ever more disastrous. Faithlessness is at the very root of our modern feelings of futility and our growing belief that the universe is, as Sam Beckett had it, merely a hostile journey from nothing to nothing.

(Poor old Sam should have attended our chapel in the Valleys instead of picking up all those daft ideas on the Left Bank. We had good ways of dealing with nutty existentialists in the Valleys and one of them was called education.)

Yet without a faith we remain, together with Sam, lost and often violent souls, anxious about our own lives and everything that there is; we become slaves to the vacuity of television and every stray nut peddling his nutty ideas; we become insatiable addicts to alcohol and sex; we are the devoted servants of Mammon and the absolute need to make the extra fiver; we are hypochondriacs who need a few pills to ease us from one painful hour to the next . . . rudderless, all of us, tossed on a sea of depression and meaninglessness because we have placed our faith in, well, nothing at all except our own self-indulgence.

For these are the days of a new and noisy wilderness well enough, populated by wandering tribes of mental midgets busy promoting worthless philosophies and bleak visions of nihilism and despair, to the extent that we are all lost in a moral chaos in which we can barely tell the difference between right and wrong, good and bad or even black and white.

Many of us vaguely hope for a new Moses to uplift and inspire us except that he would certainly end up stoned to death by the mental midgets in just the same way as they killed every new prophet that God sent to Jerusalem. Many of us merely hope for anything at all. Anything!

Old Caradoc retains his faith because he needs to retain his faith; he believes because he has to believe; he keeps nursing hope in his heart because he needs to remain hopeful. Without the scaffolding of his faith he too would see nothing but chaos and become a lost, violent soul, mollifying his anxieties with drink and drugs and hourly wondering for how much longer this painful and terrifying tedium of a useless life had to grind on until it reached the pointless conclusion of a meaningless death.

But he believes instead and keeps praying only that God will keep helping his unbelief.

THE MASTER MECHANIC

I have long admired the way that God, rather like the master mechanic, can sometimes strip you down, give you a swift service and then put you back together again.

Unbelievers will, of course, regard this statement as nonsense, which is their bad luck, but there have been quite a few times in my life when, in answer to prayer, the Master Mechanic has, in a manner of speaking, replaced my plugs, sorted out my tappets and got me up and running again.

The last time this happened was early last year when, after the death of a close and much-loved relative, my grief was as endless as it was inconsolable. The real problem with death is its non-negotiable finality and the way that God also always seems so distant and cold at the time. Nothing, you know, will ever be quite the same and your own life can start seeming pretty pointless too.

We all know of people who try and escape this pointlessness by reaching for the bottle and then end up with a greater sense of pointlessness, particularly after they've sobered up.

The only possible way of dealing with grief is to live with it and try remembering the words of the Psalmist who told us that the Lord is always near the broken-hearted and will save the crushed in spirit. This rescue will always happen in unexpected ways and at unexpected times; the holy cavalry always seems to come charging to the rescue when you are deep in the pit of despair and the pain has become all but unbearable.

Indeed, the grief over the loss of my much-loved relative lasted quite a few weeks and it was so thick and severe that parts of me kept going to sleep and I was often unable to walk any-where at all. One day an arm went dead and no sooner had that got better than a leg went. I even began thinking of it as my revolving rigor mortis and there was one moment when I thought my tongue was going to freeze up too.

All that was until one morning when I was standing at my

bedroom window watching a bird fluttering through a grey sky and I felt what I can only describe as a falling away.

This was not one of my visions but a cool, almost trance-like state in which, first of all, nothing at all moved in my mind. We all of us have a million and one things constantly moving through our minds all day long but, just now, there was nothing moving anywhere at all except a total blank. My whole consciousness was what the philosopher Locke would call a *tabula rasa*.

Then every part of my body seemed to fall away and I was just, well, spirit, hanging there in the air with no visible means of support except perhaps the warm and loving hands of God. I did see a floating halo, which is a sure sign of holy activity in my life, and heard some distant music but largely there was no sound at all, not even domestic ones.

I may have remained like this for five minutes – or even half an hour – before I was fully returned to myself and my body while I was then left with an incredible feeling of lightness and even a sense of laughter for the first time for ages. I didn't even feel the normal aches and pains of old age and could easily have managed a little tap dance around the bedroom. Every act there is – even death – leads to yet more life, I had been told. Despair will, in the end, lead to a deepening sense of joy.

Well, I knew what this was all about. This was another of my moments of renewal. The Master Mechanic had finally taken a look at a breaking-down motor and given Old Caradoc a quick 20,000-mile service before putting him back on the road again.

This facility is open to all all believers since the Master Mechanic is prepared and willing to service those who ask. He's far better at it than Toyota too even if the only real drawback is that he always works in his own time and his own way. You can't just roll up and demand immediate attention, although, when you do get looked at, the work is always first rate, free of charge and even without the normal VAT.

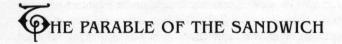# THE PARABLE OF THE SANDWICH

I was sitting in the sunshine outside the Hayes Coffee Stall the other day – as I always like to do when I'm in Cardiff – enjoying a cup of coffee and a tomato sandwich when what I can only describe as a smelly bundle of rags came and sat down at the table with me.

Everything about him spoke of defeat, from his unshaven face to the dull lustre of his eyes, the down-turned, dribbling mouth and the trembling fingers of his torn hands. He indicated that he would like the remaining half of my tomato sandwich so I gave it to him.

I asked him how he'd managed to get into that state and he told me the usual story of how he'd been in prison many times, almost always for burglary. I asked him if he had ever managed to get away with anything. No, not once, he said. Every time he had stolen anything he had always got caught. 'Well, you've just stolen my tomato sandwich and got away with it,' I pointed out but he didn't get the joke.

We chatted some more and, although he spoke quite well and even claimed to have a few 'O' levels, it was clear that this man was an out-and-out loser. Nothing had ever gone his way and nothing ever would. He added he doubted he would survive the coming winter out in the streets although, in the past, he had sometimes resorted to throwing a brick through a police station window in order to book himself a warm cell for the night. 'They came tearing out the front door, they did, an' I was just there waiting for them with open arms.'

It is always difficult for a Christian like me, who keeps trying to make sense of an ancient faith in a modern world, to know quite how he should react to men like this. We can try and care for them; we can always give them a fiver – or even half a tomato sandwich – but we always know that it is going to make no difference at all.

Nothing I could ever do was going to stop him dying and his body turning blue in some derelict house one cold night soon. Nothing at all. Men like this are beyond everyone's reach.

But, the more I thought about it, the more I came to understand that this man wasn't really a lot different from a lot of other people who would, at least on the face of it, seem a lot better off. This man had clearly never resisted his perennial temptation to steal what was not his and so he had paid the appalling cost both in terms of a blighted career and life. Yet our newspapers are always full of stories of other people whose lives are similarly ruined because they could not resist temptation in one form or another.

Royals, bishops, councillors, politicians, doctors . . . here they come, day after day, week after week and page after page, the whole, gaudy, self-important gang of them, shuffling this way and stumbling that, throwing up their hands and bleating their endless lies and pathetic excuses, all of them ruined either morally or financially or socially, just like that man on the Hayes, because at some important juncture in their lives they couldn't say no; they just couldn't resist temptation. They all gave in. 'I can resist everything but temptation,' laughed Oscar Wilde and we all know what happened to him.

The Christian narrative essentially stems from two men – Adam, who gave in, and Christ, the continually tempted one, who held on. The one put himself into a flight which became increasingly out of control and crash-landed outside Eden. The other followed the flight plan to the letter and finally flew to triumph at Calvary.

The one real call on the Christian is that he keeps resisting any and all temptation to evil, even when the world all around seems to be succumbing to it on a grand scale. We must always remain steadfast in the face of our eternal weakness, with confidence in God and his best intentions for us. Within this steadfastness we will always be winners.

And remember, my friends, it is always far better to give half a tomato sandwich on the Hayes Island than to beg for one. Never forget.

Halloween Madness

I don't quite know where they have all sprung from – or why – but suddenly our television screens have become awash with programmes about the supernatural.

We now have a whole screaming swarm of people and things, according to the television listings; aliens kidnapping people in their spaceships, time travellers whizzing back through the centuries and other assorted maniacs screaming ancient curses which, of course, come true as someone's head turns into a turnip or something equally unlikely.

It doesn't stop there either since we also have evil poltergeists and spoon-benders, we have demented astrologers peering into foggy crystal balls and specialists in automatic writing, we have werewolves lost in space and ghosts who can't find their way home. And never forget the housewife whose washing machine – clearly a Zanussi – kept sucking all the life out of her.

Now Halloween is on us again next week and our children will be running around in blood-curdling vampire masks again, banging on doors and demanding money with menaces or else throwing eggs or bags of flour at passing cars.

All this nonsense is purely an invention of American television, of course; another fashion which, like mugging, our youth learned from their screens and then went and acted out on the streets.

Halloween is a pagan festival which falls on the eve of All Saints Day. As a festival it has never had any Christian significance since it was merely another rite of the mad Druids who believed in such things as the transmigration of souls or that the mistletoe was the sacred soul of a tree. But then all the hucksters and charlatans – of whom I have been complaining – got hold of this festival and, lo, we now have a new excuse for vandalism and extortion, for assaulting people and making their lives a misery.

Yet I have to grant that, in its glorification of fangs and loutishness, in its love of weird behaviour Halloween is now a real rite for our time. Just look at your child in his mask with fangs dripping with blood and bags of flour which he is going to hurl at someone and say, yes, this truly is a child of our times. This is a child for whom I sweated hard all my life raising in the values and shadow of the junk that is almost all American television.

The people who promote the supernatural are all fakes who are in it for the money. Everything they claim to be true is false – even most of their names – and it is difficult, if not impossible, to validate almost anything they do or say.

The supernatural view is in complete contrast to the teachings of biblical Christianity; this view denies any notion of a personal God, emphasizing man as being the author of his own divinity and rejecting all claims of morality. The lie of the serpent was: 'You will all be gods.' The good is no different from the bad, in the supernatural view. The lie has the same standing as the truth.

The supernatural, then, has become a modern religion and Halloween has become the most sacred day for its followers. The supernatural is a pseudo-religion based on gullibility and ignorance; it affirms lies as truth while also affirming the sovereignty of the devil as the arch-deceiver.

All such deception and lies should have been destroyed on Calvary, of course, but, not only have they not been destroyed, they are thriving in every home and on every street corner, particularly on the day of Halloween.

Open your doors to the trick or treaters next Thursday night then; open your doors and behold the children you took out of the life of the chapels and left to die in front of your televisions. Open your doors and weep as you remember how you abandoned all parental responsibilities and left those trick or treaters in a flickering glow of death as you scampered off down the pub.

A MIGHTY MAN OF GOD

The most influential religious leader in the modern world is undoubtedly Dr Billy Graham and I was interested to learn that he last preached in Wales almost exactly fifty years ago, in 1946, when his tour included Gorseinon, Cardiff and that Sodom and Gomorrah of the Valleys, Pontypridd.

I didn't see him then but I did once in the early eighties in Bristol and regard him quite simply as a mighty man of God who has considerably enriched the earth and all her peoples.

Many have been suspicious of the emotion behind his revivalism but there has surely always been a place for feelings in services. But Dr Graham did not anyway orchestrate the wild swings of emotion largely found in Evan Roberts' revival of 1904. Dr Graham's tools were a plain, forceful sermon, a sound biblical message and a call for personal repentance.

I saw him one dull afternoon in Ashton Gate football stadium in Bristol in 1984. About a hundred photographers were milling around a huge, beflowered stage on the pitch and a red carpet stretched right across the half-way line. The 2,000-strong choir began by singing 'All Hail the Power of Jesu's Name'.

The atmosphere was amazing, even a little like the National Stadium's half an hour before the kick-off of a rugby international. Great spasms of emotion wheeled around and around the crowds on the packed terraces. Isolated chants broke out. 'We are here to welcome Billy back,' a man said into the microphone. 'Many of us think he belongs here.' More cheers and chants.

George Hamilton V sang the opening song and then Dr Graham stepped up and began his sermon with these words: 'I want to speak to you as if this is the last sermon that I will ever proclaim. May we be conscious of no one except God. For God so loved the world that he gave his only begotten son that whosoever (and that includes you) should not perish but have everlasting life.'

As the sermon unfolded his words were soft and involving. There were no shouts or hysterical outbursts but the tone did become slightly more urgent. That old oratorical magic was clearly still magical. Occasionally the hand was raised and the finger always pointed at *you*.

He was surprisingly tall with ravishing blue eyes and a pro-nounced hunch in his shoulders. His nose had immense, Concorde-like proportions and his gingerish hair was long at the back and reached down over his shirt collar. The Bible was never far from his hand and then he furnished his famous invitation. 'So now I am going to ask you to get up out of your seats . . . '

Then, with the organ sorrowing softly, they really did begin getting up out of their seats, singly at first but then in twos, threes, and some 2,352 came forward that afternoon, we learned later.

Well, our chapel group thought it was all pretty exciting and many spoke of the way the American had pressed a lot of their spiritual buttons. He certainly won the great respect of Old Caradoc who was even on the point of wheezing up out of his own seat but, for some reason, didn't.

Yet even great American evangelists cannot last forever and I have heard that Dr Graham is these days quite ill and will undoubtedly be surrounded by a vast blanket of the world's prayers.

There must be now, however, a great opportunity for someone to step into his shoes and we do need another man like him. In the wake of Dunblane and other random killings and shootings even the dimmest are now understanding that we are seeing nothing less than the wholesale moral destruction of our society. We will all soon, as T. S. Eliot had it, be killing one another in the streets.

Dark times have again and again found new leaders, so the only real question now is: where is the new Billy?

A PATRON SAINT OF RATS

I gave the oration at a small Valleys funeral recently for a man who, in all truth, wasn't that much of a man because he was almost always drunk and gambled far too much.

In fact he was the proverbial waste of space who didn't have a lot going for him at all – except for the fact that he could drink a pint of beer without moving his Adam's apple – so I had to struggle quite hard to think of anything positive to say about him at all. You simply can't denounce a man at his funeral even if I've often been tempted to try. But then I remembered his one lone act of goodness, even if he was drunk as a wheel at the time.

Our much-mourned brother, I recalled, was standing at Cardiff Railway Station late one night many years ago, full of hiccups and happiness, waiting for a train which wasn't showing up when he noticed a few dozen cages containing rats which were being sent to somewhere like Porton Down for experimental purposes.

Without further ado he let the lot out, causing bedlam on the crowded platform and even bigger bedlam when he got home since he had also taken one back in his jacket pocket to show his poor, long-suffering wife.

There was then considerable surprise at his funeral service, in the shape of dropping jaws and raising heads, when I went on to say that our brother was, in fact, in some ways, an unsung saint of the Valleys since, when he released those doomed rats, he was doing nothing less than celebrating the very foundation stone of the Celtic church.

Had St Cuthbert or St Columba or St David or indeed any other of the great Celtic saints been waiting at Cardiff Railway Station for a late train to the Valleys which wasn't showing up then they would almost certainly have done the same thing, I added. For these old saints embraced every living thing with a holy fervour. Cuthbert was always pals with his seals and David was in an almost permanent conversation with that dove on his shoulder which, in some senses, was one of our first management consultants.

The veneration for the natural world was a primary belief of the Celtic Church which first taught us about the purity and sacredness of all living things; the heaven that is in a wild flower; the freedom that is in a flying bird and the way the very spirit of God holds together even the wildest landscapes and allows everything in it to thrive. The natural world is the greatest and most formidable balancing act known to man or his imagination.

Indeed, the very first symbol of the Holy Spirit in the Celtic Church was the wild goose and what is more ravishing than watching an arrowhead of geese flying free, parting the sky and calling out to one another. Geese are also faithful birds who pair for life, mourn a dead partner and care devotedly for their young.

Even the robin got his red breast at Calvary, he once told St Columba. There was a particular thorn which was causing Jesus a lot of pain so the bird pulled it out and the subsequent splash of blood on his breast has stayed there ever since.

The very fields all around us were where the bread was broken and the wine poured. All early worship in the Celtic Church took place out of doors where prayers mingled with the rain and the liturgy was chanted to the calls of the wild birds.

So I was, in this way, able to make a reasonable fist of my oration and commend the spirit of the man we had just lost if only because he released a load of rats one dark night on Cardiff Railway Station. The oration wasn't totally convincing, of course, since everyone there knew him but my words did at least prove that in every drunken wastrel's life there is always something, somewhere, that is useful, good and kind, even if, at first, it sometimes takes ages to think of it.

An Angel for Advent

I drove out to the Heads of the Valleys the other day where I like to walk high in the hills and look down on the small townships while also enjoying the brooding calm of the countryside.

This is the time of Advent, four weeks which will lead up to a new Christian year and the land, with all the damp and grey hues, is perfect for those moments of quiet contemplation we all need before the full horror of yet another commercial Christmas hits us.

The days start grey in this time of Advent and generally remain grey throughout the afternoon until they merely fade away tiredly. Only the odd bird seemed to be up and about as I walked, with nothing stirring in the wet, squelching mud. There is a general sense of keening on such afternoons; a feeling of tense anticipation perhaps which can turn to hope and even a visionary fervour.

The grey skies were watchful as I walked on down a path next to a farm. The river, swollen by a few days of rain, was flowing faster than usual and a few sheep looked at me. We can sense something of the creation of the world on such afternoons of late autumnal quiet. There is also something of the mystery of God in all this stillness too. It was out of such stillness that God brought forth life.

We need also to focus our thoughts on the coming of Christ at Advent; we need to remember that his most repeated promise to us was that he would return. 'When I come back to you,' he said. 'I will not leave you as orphans.'

We know that his spirit has never really left the world and that he is here with us for all time but we also know that our world is becomingly increasingly stained by a most dramatic outbreak of evil; an evil which is even now attacking every family and home; an evil which can surely only now be beaten back by the return of the Son of Man.

So in these long, grey days of Advent, when the darkness never really seems to leave us, Christians everywhere should be waiting, hoping and praying that darkness will not be the final word. We should be preparing our thoughts and hearts and not, under any circumstances, be taken by surprise.,

I came to the brow of another hill and, looking down on my slumbering people in our blighted Valley homes, I lifted my arms up high when I saw a huge angel come gliding down through the cold, grey skies. My whole face was smothered with a luminous warmth and I merely waved at it as a child might wave a little flag at the Queen.

Many people don't believe in angels and many more have never seen one. But Old Caradoc has seen them often and believed in them all his life. The early Celtic Church always taught the reality of angels and here was another again, cruising the Valley skies with a careless and beautiful rapture, moving this way and that on great golden wings of fire.

Angels have always been God's messengers or ambassadors and there are untold thousands of them working in different parts of the world in a carefully structured army led by the Archangel Michael. They will all be fully mobilized, the Bible tells us, on the day of Christ's return, on the plains of Armageddon, when they will do battle with all the angels of hell.

So the sight of my brilliant angel on that grey Valley afternoon told me that, while my defeated people have forgotten God, then God has not forgotten them. Those great wings of fire also told me that these long grey hours of Advent may get stormy and colourful and that all early moves to drive God from his throne really will be firmly repulsed by the transcendent brilliance of the Second Coming.

Acts of Repentance

I knew a woman who found herself lying drunk in a field in Porthcawl. She was barely able to move and just lay there, listening to the voices and laughter of the people and children walking past her. Tears began falling as she asked herself why couldn't she be like everyone else? What was the matter with her? Why was she in this mess?

Even as she asked herself these questions she could feel

something stirring deep inside her. She was finding a will to resist her formidable addiction; she was feeling those first golden moments of repentance when everything would change and her life would come back to her anew.

I knew another man who ended up living in a cave in Penarth. He was in a soiled, mad condition, drinking rough cider or meths, and, of course, he blamed everyone else for his fallen state. One night he heard the sound of dogs and believed they were out hunting for him. He kept thinking of his relatives at his funeral who were all going to be weeping copiously because they had let him down.

Yet one night he was seeing his relatives all gathered around his grave again when, right out of the blue, he saw that they were all sighing with relief and laughing their heads off. The fault was with him and him only. It was up to him to sort himself out and it was with that one simple insight that he had a change of heart and began getting well again.

When an adulterer ends up getting trapped in emotional bonds with someone else we also frequently find that the only release from this appalling plight comes when the adulterer makes a full confession both to God and the wronged partner. Everything that is fine in Christianity – love, forgiveness, reconciliation – can then come into play. Lives and the family can be unified again. The hurts can start healing although they may take time. Happiness again becomes a possibility but only when there has been repentance first.

We all know tales of the most unlikely people who have carried an unreal burden of guilt until that one great moment when they have finally managed to unload it and truly repent of the original crime. We also all know of the most devastating consequences that have often ensued when some have become trapped in their pride and greed, ending up with colossally expensive court cases for everyone. They found themselves stuck in the track; they wouldn't turn back; they wouldn't repent of it.

But repentance doesn't quite stop there. To be truly significant, amends have to be made or apologies offered, no matter if they might come twenty years later. These amends must, without fail, be made. Also be prepared to look out for new roads when the old roads fail. Always remain flexible and ready to take the hard option.

So don't wait for the earthquake which you know is going to come. Don't sit around waiting for the police or the bankruptcy court. Don't just carry on hoping the wife or husband won't find out. Repent of what you've done with a broken and contrite heart. Start making amends immediately, no matter how difficult or even expensive that may be. This is the Path of the Cross; the only path that ever leads to happiness or freedom.

Repentance is at the very heart of the Christian Mystery and you can be sure that God will always offer times of refreshing but only when you show that you have truly and honestly repented.

So if you find the flame of repentance in your heart then cherish and nurture it. This light may well lead you out of a painful and lonely darkness. This light will do nothing less than take you into a golden new world of hope in which happiness is the norm of some fleeting feeling usually touched only briefly when you are very drunk.

THE STAINS OF SIN

I keep having a powerful and recurring dream of late which involves a rather marvellous giant with big feet.

This giant of mine spends his days wandering over a great plain full of white mists which keep turning red at the edges. But, every so often, he finds he cannot move around properly so he stops and takes out his heart which has blackened with sin.

He then washes his heart carefully in a freshwater spring, cleaning it up and making it nice and new. The heart is popped back into his chest and he is on his way again. Just like that.

Listening to someone else's dreams, I have long believed, is often almost as boring as listening to their dirty jokes but there is a powerful Celtic symbolism about this dream which I find quite pleasing.

The freshwater spring would represent the cleansing power of water which is also the bringer and giver of all life. The Celts of old knew all about the value and importance of pure water long before the Greens made it one of their main battle cries. People were always being cured of all sorts of maladies with the aid of pure water – even those as grave as losing their heads – in Celtic mythology.

But I also like the way that this fresh water washed away my giant's sins. Sin is a curiously devalued and even old-fashioned word but it has always had a real and important status in the Christian canon.

Sin is not only a wrong act but a state of alienation from God. It points to a clear collapse in our love relationship with God and the way we keep betraying him with our increasingly corrupt hearts. Sin is a state of enmity with God; a malignant power which can keep us enslaved all our long days through.

We have all – everyone of us – become stained by sin and it has come to the point when I can see it almost everywhere I look, particularly and especially in myself.

I see such features as hardness of heart, pride, sensuality, fear, greed, lust and, most importantly, our continued and stubborn unwillingness to open our hearts to God. I see my own Welsh tribe becoming ever more self-indulgent and venal almost by the hour; a tribe which has become literally lost as it wanders a desert almost completely of its own making. Then there are the other more collective and international sins like sexism, ageism, racism and imperialism. These are the sins which do not allow people to grow in their own light; sins which interfere with their natural growth.

The Bible tells us on a number of times that we are inherently sinful. The Psalmist told of those who err from the womb, speaking lies. We are from the moment we are born, in other words, enmeshed in an almost constant fight with the mystery of evil. And it is to fight that evil – both in others but especially in ourselves – that is one of the most basic challenges of The Cross.

So we must use the inspiration of The Cross and the leadership of the man who died on it to fight our many and varied tragic flaws. We will never quite eliminate them but, with some serious and prayerful effort, we might at least keep them under control.

This calls for a constant state of vigilance and a readiness to examine our every thought and motive although how much easier it would be if we could take out our hearts, like my giant, and simply wash them clean of every disabling impurity. Then pop them back in and get on our way.

GLUE-SNIFFERS IN THE CHAPEL

The winter frosts have bitten into the earth hard with only a few hours of thin, cold sunshine if we are lucky. This cold plays hell with my old bones and I still haven't quite shaken off my gloom after returning from Jerusalem.

There's a reign of undiluted evil over the Valleys these days which, in every way and almost every hour, seems to be getting worse. I have barely been able to believe the evidence of my eyes as I've seen wholesale fights breaking out in shopping centres, young girls falling drunkenly into gutters and windows being broken pointlessly.

I'm also finding more and more that I can actually see all our modern demons mingling among the shoppers; the killers of American films, the massing spirits of those hateful video shops and the black rays of the satellite dishes demonizing every home and hearth.

All these things which I have kept telling you about have all but killed my people and destroyed their faith; all these active agents of evil have eaten into the very heart and mind of God and let no one tell you otherwise.

Old Caradoc has now taken to spending more and more time in his deserted chapel high on the hill. This building, broken as it is, helps me to connect with the past and the values which made us great. We could stand tall and look anyone in the eye then.

Here, in my chapel, I can still pick up snatches of great preaching in the darkness; I can still hear great waves of prayer and praise in a truly worshipping community come together in pure adoration, the lifting up of the redeemed spirit towards God in mass contemplation of his holy perfection.

Corporate worship was always the moral and creative heart of a Valley community but there's hardly much of that anymore which is why our communities are all but being destroyed by crime, violence and drugs.

The last service I attended in a neighbouring valley had a child rolling around on a football in front of the altar. Another actually got into the pulpit while the preacher was delivering his sermon while his parents smirked proudly and a drunk behind me snored his way through the whole proceedings.

So, unable to face the horrors of the present, I dwell a lot on the past and, sometimes, God talks to me too and tells me of his deep and bitter anguish at the way all the tribes of the world are now stumbling into a long and endless night of faithlessness and violence.

He goes on about this a lot and there are many moments when I find his sadness almost unbearable although, when I ask why he doesn't do anything about it, he generally falls silent.

It was very cold on the last night I sat with God in my lonely chapel and perhaps I hadn't closed the door properly behind me but three youngsters got in there. I was shrouded in darkness in my favourite corner and said nothing as they moved about, trying to break things or pull off fittings or shouting obscenities. Finally they settled down on the dais in front of the pulpit and began sniffing on something which may have been a pot of glue, occasionally giggling as they passed it between them.

But, even so, I remained quiet; I remained a dark, silent shadow deep in the darkness. Perhaps it has got that I can no longer feel any real outrage and perhaps it is that I have witnessed this so many times before. Here was the seed of my great forefathers sitting here destroying themselves before their young lives had begun; here, in a sense, was the end of all of us.

So I continued sitting there and recalled those distant nights of prayer and praise; I heard the flow of a majestic sermon and I did absolutely nothing as I remained stock-still, a grieving God at my shoulder, and feeling only hot tears rolling silently down my cold cheeks.

OUR LONG WINTER WAIT

There's a mood of emptiness and longing in our hearts in these times of ice and cold. We look to our dead plants wondering if there is any life in them. We scan the rock-hard earth for signs of these first small green spears of growth.

But there is nothing anywhere, except this cold from which

there seems to be no escape, even in our beds. The icy wind keeps blowing on flat harmonicas in the eaves and I was amused to find myself dreaming about the sands of Barry Island the other night with buckets and spades and the whole of my back falling apart with sunburn.

Out on the valley slopes it's the same desperate story, the sheep searching about for food and shelter, the triangular footprints of birds in the snow and the huge swathes of powdered ice which looks set on staying there until next Christmas. When people speak on the corners, their warm breath makes their mouths plume like so many gossiping dragons.

There's also a sense of evil and death around the place in these times of snow; a few more old age pensioners have gone down with hypothermia, yet more victims of a government's niggardly refusal to give them their basic right of warmth. You couldn't keep a budgie warm with their heat allowances.

Almost everyone seems to be swigging Night Nurse and have runny noses so we are all trying to keep our heads well down in this freezing valley of ours and we wait for the sun.

But waiting is not always such a bad thing. Jesus told his disciples to wait in the city for the arrival of the Holy Spirit. We must also wait on God and put our trust in his immaculate sense of timing; we must keep bleeding with prayer as we wait for whatever it is that we think we want. Remember the Psalmist who cried: 'I waited patiently for the Lord's help, then he listened to me and heard me cry.'

There have been times without number when Old Caradoc has got into deep difficulties and then waited patiently for God to hear his cry. At first these prayers rarely seemed to be answered and, yet again, I felt something of God's own coldness and deafness.

But, in time, the fruit of the prayer was given me and it was often nothing like I had been asking for – only better. I'm told this often happens when people buy houses; they suffer grave disappointment when they don't get what they want and then end up with a far better one.

There is an art to waiting and this art is something we can practise and develop every day in our bus queues, post offices and banks. This art puts us back in the real world; it will enable us to deal better with the disintegration we see all around; it will even reinforce our sense of democracy and feelings for our fellow man.

Waiting always brings its own peculiar sense of reward. Disappointment is rare for the person who really understands the art of waiting and knows that perhaps he has not waited long enough.

So many of us in the Valley are standing around in a cold, bitter night waiting for that first brilliant kiss of the sun. We are like Joshua looking up at the mountains longing for a turn in the weather. We are waiting for the daybreak which we often fear deep in our hearts will not arrive.

But it will, my people. Hold fast to your faith and keep a candle of hope held high in this long, cold night. Wait in faith, in love and, most of all, in readiness since, in time, God will reveal his hand and everything that your heart has ever longed for will be given to you.

TALKING IN PRAYER

I was having a quiet snooze in my favourite armchair the other afternoon, *The Western Mail* on my knees and my stockinged feet warming by the fire, when I woke speaking in tongues. I often pray aloud in tongues when I am not sure what I'm praying for but this was the first time I have done so in my sleep.

Out the words flowed in a fervent, unstoppable stream, nothing making much sense and as if I was standing at the Pearly Gates and delivering a heart-felt petition directly to God on behalf of the Welsh. There was certainly a lot of urgency in my words – and no little anxiety since my eyes were flooding with tears.

Mrs Caradoc did what she always does at times like this: left me alone and went off into the kitchen to make me a cup of tea. She has developed a wonderful sense of strategy over the years and nothing much surprises her any more.

When I had finished my prayer of tongues and tears I relaxed in my armchair and felt strangely replenished, the usual effect that prayer has on me. In a sense, my life has become one long, secret prayer and this was merely another, albeit emotional, side to it.

In prayer we develop our relationship with the many-splendoured heart of God and there is not one second of any one day when we cannot reach out and touch him. Prayer is the soul of faith, as John Calvin had it. Without it our faith becomes lifeless and dies.

We can pray anywhere at all, in the holy ground of our homes, gardens or work places or even, if the mood takes us, in our empty churches and chapels. My best prayer time always takes place in the bath, particularly after I have washed myself and the water has drained away. The Moslems are always washing themselves before prayer and there is more than a touch of Moslem in Old Caradoc.

You can send out flash prayers at people in the street, enveloping them in the love of Christ, and even send these prayers flooding into buildings, purifying the very walls. You can transmit this love even in a handshake as your mind busily tries to wrap the world in a chrysalis of prayer.

Many simple prayers are manipulative requests and there is something to this but we must not pray for ourselves. The principal point of prayer is that God's kingdom may be continually extended although there is nothing that is beyond the scope of prayer. Moses even prayed that God would change his mind. In prayer we can even wrestle with God himself, lay our anger and complaint at his feet.

In times of anxiety and distress it is good and useful to stand there and go through the Lord's Prayer, one slow word at a time, thinking of each and every word. This practice is far more effective than valium and has never failed to calm me down and make me stronger. Martin Luther invited prayerful and regular meditations on the Ten Commandments.

But when you do pray and find, along with R. S. Thomas, the untenanted cross, the long silence, the *Deus Absconditus,* do not give up or despair. Wait in faith and trust and everything will emerge in the right way and in God's own time.

We should keep building up new patterns of prayer and making them the heart of our lives. It is only through prayer that we will become a nation of mystics and prophets again, reunited with an attentive and loving Father who will then lead us out of this violent and destructive wilderness.

God listens to our prayers; they are his food and right through which he grows with his children. He wants us as love partners, not slaves. Prayer is the telephone line with which we talk to God and he to us. Yes, it's good to pray.

€MPTY VESSELS

The sight of a lonely preacher in his pulpit droning on about something deeply obscure to a congregation of half a dozen old ladies – and a deaf dog – has always filled me with the deepest gloom.

But when you actually listen to this lonely preacher going on about all the sunshine angels of his candy floss heaven and, if not them, the flames and darkness and heat of the hobs of hell, you get even gloomier and wonder why even these half a dozen old ladies bothered to turn up. The dog at least has a good excuse.

For surely this is one of the main reasons why our churches and chapels are so empty: not so much that we are living in a sinful, faithless age but that many of our preachers still insist in talking to us in an obsolete language about redundant concepts which probably never had any meaning.

These men are empty vessels, full of sound and fury, signifying nothing. In terms of the Church, they are quite literally useless and should have been pensioned off years ago, in much the same savage way they are now pruning our best and most experienced teachers.

But they don't get pensioned off. The useless ones are always left alone and we, the hungry sheep, look up waiting to be fed and all that happens is our minds wander over everything as our hearts turn cold with boredom. We count our toes. We try to remember what's on the television. We can't work out why the milkman has always disliked us. We wonder if this sermon is going to continue until next Christmas.

I was listening to one such pulpit warrior some time ago as he busily set out his non-thoughts in a non-language, sketching the unlikely rewards we are due to get in heaven if we are good, followed, as usual, by all the terrible punishments due to befall us in hell if we are bad. The detail was all there as if he had made a personal inspection of both places. On no account whatsoever, he warned, were we to be bad.

I thought this piffle went out of fashion along with Bombazine bloomers but there it was and, for all most knew, this man could be talking in Klingon to a gang of half-wits who had just stumbled out on to Dowlais Top from a space ship from Mars.

The church is brilliant at complaining about what's wrong with the world but we rarely hear what's wrong with the Church. Here, surely, was a prime example. There was no real conviction in this man's words, there was nothing of himself and not even any pictures from the life of Christ. All we had was flannel without end, vague ideas in a vague language, doubtless drummed into his head in Sunday School and repeated without any real thought ever since.

Heaven is not the distant abstraction he was presenting but something we can discover in the here and now; a state in which it is possible to achieve a harmony, a peace and a wholeness.

We all of us have elements of good and evil battling away inside us and we alone decide what will be victorious in the way we think and act and conduct ourselves. If we fill our lives with the fragrance of God, we will know times of peace and serenity which amount to heaven. If we abandon God and all his laws, we enter a hell which is always of our own making.

Jesus was the life of heaven and if we relate closely to that life, we too can savour heaven. Every act of faith takes us closer to him and hence to heaven. Thus every sinful act takes us into the depression and loneliness of hell. Heaven, then, becomes a living movement, a humanly attainable state of grace. Hell is where love dies.

So the sooner we stop mumbling metaphysical claptrap about the hells and heavens beyond the grave, which no one really understands or relates to, the sooner people might start finding their way back to our churches and chapels again and the sooner they might be taught in proper language all the deep secrets and joys of being born again.

Food for the Soul

We are now well into Lent – that 40-day period of penitence and fasting which leads up to the great drama of Easter and I have been taking it unusually seriously.

This was the time Jesus spent in the desert, resisting temptation and preparing himself for the trials to come and so, acknowledging the increasing urgency of the times while also trying to get closer to him, I have been trying new forms of retreat built on fasting and prayer.

Breakfast is tea and two slices of toast, then I will take a drive out into the hills, wandering the woodland paths and trying to locate God in prayer. These are good times to contact God with the stirrings of fresh shoots in the earth and the new blooms whispering enthralling promises of the resurrection.

I'll have a couple of sandwiches for lunch unless it's Friday when I'll fast all day. The custom of fasting originated with those who were expecting to be baptized after being catechumens. The third, fourth and fifth Sundays of Lent refer to the process of preparing for baptism.

Fasting is a key spiritual discipline and the religious mind has long understood that discipline brings freedom and happiness. Discipline is the key component of discipleship; it brings people closer to Christ wherein they can find a proper balance in their lives. Only through prayer and fasting can we understand the various emotions that attempt to take over our lives. Only then can we recognize them and then attempt to do something about them before they enslave us.

There are no biblical commandments to fast but there are plenty of references to its practice. 'I will not be enslaved to anything,' wrote Paul. 'I pommel my body to subject it.' For him, freedom meant frequent fastings. 'I humbled my soul by fasting,' said David in the Psalms.

In the afternoon Old Caradoc will then take to his derelict chapel where he will remain the lone watchman until the twilight comes. There is much activity under the floorboards at this time of year and I have noticed the spiders have got unusually busy again. The first of the flies have been showing their noses too.

Here it helps if I light a candle on the altar and sit in the pew watching the flame hold my prayers. Candles keep our prayers alive long after we have stopped saying them. They tell us that darkness cannot be the final word; they also remind us of our intense fragility and humanity because they can easily be blown out.

Whole dramas can unfold deep in the flame if I stare into it long enough: the smiling faces of those I've loved, the tears of those I've lost, the crying babies I've stooped to pick up and comfort . . . all of them there in a flickering procession and held up in love's compact all of fire.

One afternoon a vision began coming together within the candle flame, fairly incomprehensible as most visions are, but this time consisting of a fleet of angels being chased by a ball of fire which had many fiery tails, as if it had just rolled in from some distant corner of hell itself. The fire kept charring the angels' wings and stopping them from flying away.

In the evening it will be a little light devotional reading next to the fire in the kitchen – away from the television-radiated hearth of the living room – and then a time of prayer before an early night.

So Lent, then, has become a time of withdrawal from my old social habits and an attempt to forge a new relationship with God. It is a time of sacrifice and fasting when I try to come closer to the Man of Sorrows as he prayed alone in his desert fastness.

Lent is a time when we prepare to celebrate the unique gift of life as we all look forward to lifting the Paschal flame of Easter. Jesus said: 'I am the light of the world.'

Our beloved waterman

A bleak, cold wind blowing in off the sea. A frozen landscape powdered with frost and the trumpets of the daffodils nodding in the wind. The outlying islands. A parliament of crows.

Rainbows forming in a disorderly line of brilliant colour along the coast. A great man is going to be born to you, the rainbows are saying. A holy man. A new riddle in the mind of God. A long cry of pain. A heaving of hips. A single shaft of sunlight on the mother. A bloodied head and the rapturous applause of many gathered angels. The mother's fingerprints on the stone.

A boy walks through a daffodil dale with a dove on his shoulder. The dove is explaining the deep secrets of God to the boy. He listens to every word with watchful blue eyes. Evil Druids are standing in distant oak woods and they are worried their reign might be coming to an end.

The boy becomes a man, nearly seven feet tall with the body of an ox and hands the size of shovels. Every muscle ripples as he pulls his plough through the fields. His dove still flutters concernedly around his shoulders and he stops work for a minute or so to drink water.

He eats one meal of wild leeks or herbs a day and will occasionally take a little fish. He never takes wine. Apart from work his day is built around worship and he will often pray right through the night.

This man has a strange and mystical relationship with nature. One night, at prayer, he hears a nightingale singing and the careless rapture of the song so entrances him he fears he will never be able to pray properly again since he will always be listening out for that bird. He therefore forbids the bird to ever again sing in his diocese and one never does. To this day.

Word of this man spreads through a land ruled by Druidic evil and often laid low by tornadoes carrying plague germs. Here the young die young. Mothers become barren early and the fruit withers on the vines. Is this man going to usher in a new dawn?

He becomes a man of healing and strange miracles drift out of his huge fingers like lazy flashes of the Holy Spirit. The deaf begin hearing a new dawn. The blind begin seeing it. Fruit becomes especially abundant and the mothers are fertile again.

His tongue is eloquent and, once, while denouncing a new heresy, a mound grows under his feet making his words as huge and impressive as thunder. Nothing can resist his brilliance at destructive definition or the forceful logic of his attacks. He knows and understands the enduring power of The Word.

He lives to the tremendous age of 147. 'The day is close at hand and I am glad to go the way of my fathers,' he said.

'Brothers and sisters, be cheerful and keep your faith and do the little things you have heard and seen through me.' He dies with a smile on his face and praise on his lips.

Many people actually see angels carrying him up over the Jordan. Even the Seraphim come out to greet him and the welcome home party lasts a week.

Yet he stays with us still. The body is but a husk and the personality lives forever. This man's personality and ideas live in the heart of us to this day, especially on this day, his day. We still hold his values dear and he still frames the way we regard our culture and faith. We took his little things and made them the big cornerstones of our lives.

So we can see our great and beloved Waterman still – walking across a frozen landscape powdered with frost and a bleak, cold wind blowing in off the sea. We can see him looking around with pleasure at the daffodils trumpeting the good news of his life to the wind. The outlying islands. A parliament of crows.

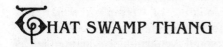

ᚦHAT SWAMP THANG

I never thought I would live to see the moment but there I was the other night standing on a dance floor with a cowboy on one side of me and a cowgirl on the other as a Country and Western band raised hell on the stage behind.

Coloured streams of light trickled over all as I goaded my old bones to step this way and that. All the dancers on the floor moved in tight formation one way and the other before, as a man, moving back again.

Mrs Caradoc was bobbing around in the middle of the dancers almost as if she had been born to it. She was something of an Isadora Duncan of Pontypridd until I came along and cast a great cloud of chapel gloom over her life, she has often said. But there she was, taking three steps up and two back, wiggling her behind this way and that, a smile as broad as the Severn Bridge, a regular rhinestone cowgirl and as happy as a kid making sandcastles in the sun on Barry Island.

Old Caradoc had taken Mrs Caradoc to a holiday camp in

Devon. But then we went to the dance there that night which turned out to be an American line dance. The first thing I noticed was the dancers – all dolled up in stetsons, bootlace ties and silver boots (and that was just the girls) – were everything from the ages of eight to eighty.

All you've got to do, we were told, was get right in the middle of them and latch onto what everyone else was doing. That's what we did, except I quickly ran out of puff but Mrs Caradoc looked as though she was going to keep going at least until next Christmas.

It was marvellous fun while my body lasted out doing, I think, dances like the Rattlesnake Shuffle or That Swamp Thang. There's about four hundred steps in line dancing but, as long as you keep jigging about and keep a wary eye on everyone else, you've got a fifty-fifty chance of not being trampled by a bopping army of moving line dancers.

I've long had a soft spot for Country and Western music with its bouncy, duelling banjos and loopy lyrics which are always going on about a strange mixture of weepin' or walkin' tall. Women are all women who dress up like Cindy dolls and stand by their men in the country and western code. The men are all men with their big muscles and good manners and simple Southern philosophies. Line dancing is for ageing rockers since, fortunately, you don't have to do too much except stay out of everyone else's way.

Mrs Caradoc is right, in a sense, about the chapel's love of all things gloomy, of course. The chapel never quite knew what to make of dancing after John Wesley said that, yes, of course, there could be dancing but it should be men with men, women with women, in daylight and outdoors.

We have no record of Jesus line dancing, unfortunately, but we can be sure that he loved to celebrate the holiness and beauty of the human body. There was nothing of a prude about him and it is nothing less than shocking that so many of his so-called followers seem to feel the need to go around dressed in sombre clothes with starch in their hearts and their heads in a bucket.

Dance is both primordial and universal. There are some who believe that dance is the origin of religion, helping people to relate to nature through ecstasy and aesthetics. The Hindus have their own god, the Lord of the Dance, who creates, sustains and destroys.

People show the wild gladness of their hearts when they dance. They are saying yes to their humanity and their most basic emotions. Dance is a basic affirmation of human creation and, even in our lowest moments when our shackles are at their heaviest, we should always remember the example of Our Saviour and then get up and dance with joy.

THE SECRETS OF DEATH

My whole body was full of pain and stress the other night; pain from the variety of aches that gather like flies around the old and stress from all the fires that the young keep lighting out on the Valley slopes.

I can't help believing that these fires mean something and that the young are telling us in a vivacious way about their loss too. There are even moments when I feel we are in hell already; a hell where love has become impossible and pain is the norm.

Anyway sleep kept eluding me and I was just lying there in the flickering darkness being serenaded by Mrs Caradoc's snores when I had the strangest sensation that something was trying to escape from my body.

Just then my whole being, which might have been my soul, simply stepped up out of my body and began walking towards the bedroom door. The one thing I immediately noticed about this new release of mine was that, for the first time for years, I was free of all pain and stress.

When I opened the bedroom door I stepped out onto a large arena of pure light. This light was devoid of anything except light. I had never seen anything like it since there seemed to be no shadows or texture in it. There was an odd sort of music playing too – a delightful sound but not exactly musical in the sense that it didn't seem to have any discernible notes.

As I continued moving around in this light I decided that this must be a much longed-for premonition of death and here I was being shown something of the dark secret that has eluded us all.

Light which is nothing but light. Music which is not exactly music. Not staggering revelations but something to work on; a small insight which may well lead to a larger one.

The first theologians used to teach that, after death, there is nothing at all. The breath returns to air and the body to dust. The emphasis was always on the positive aspects of *this* life.

The Christian Church took this a lot further, of course, teaching that our friendship with God could continue beyond death. The faithful could look forward to a resurrection of their spirit in the same way as Jesus staged a resurrection after dying on the Cross. Christian thought, then, developed on the twin premises of a soul and a resurrected body. Immortality was something that belonged to God alone.

So Christ breaks the power of death over us and, through him, our soul or body can enter heaven where we will feel a continuity with our present body. Here all our tears will be wiped away and we will forever feed on the majesty and splendour of God.

What is heaven actually like? We have a few biblical clues such as that it will be a 'heavenly Jerusalem' which, hopefully, means that it will be nothing like the mess that is the present earthly Jerusalem. Heaven will also have authority over cities and here the redeemed of the earth will learn new songs.

But such clues are as vague as they are imprecise. My best guess is that the concept of heaven is beyond human understanding. Yet, on the evidence of my premonition, the whole place will be full of pure light without shadows. There will also be music which is not musical in any formal sense.

After a short tour of this celestial arena I stepped back into my bedroom and body and was soon full of the old aches and pains again, lying there wondering why the whole might of modern medicine can't come up with something to stop Mrs Caradoc snoring. This woman has never lost five minutes' sleep in her life. Even on the day Chamberlain declared war on Germany she was asleep and snoring as soon as her head touched that pillow.

$\mathcal{S}$OUNDS OF SUMMER

It was one of those strange, warm nights in the Valley that we often get at the start of summer with shivers of foreign winds and distant storms threatening but failing to break.

Blazing angry eyes kept appearing and disappearing in the darkness. Odd cries of pain seared the shadows and light veils of something cobwebby kept brushing lightly against your cheeks. Those cries of pain again.

But you felt no fear in this shifting, crackling night because you just knew that everything in the natural world was up and about just now, doing whatever they need to do in their various holes, webs or tree trunks.

Those blazing eyes would belong to the foxes coming down the Valley slopes in increasing numbers to forage in our dustbins. Bees have begun swarming in the eaves of my roof again and the flowers are standing tall in gaudy display.

The trick on such summer nights is to let your senses run riot in the air and soon you will feel at one with the natural world and everything that is working so busily all around you. When you make that connection you will also connect with God, currently working flat-out on a 24-hour day as he pumps furious smelts of creative energy into every single nook and cranny of his great creation.

These are the weeks that he has been preparing himself for all the year around and now, with his shirt sleeves rolled up and huge rivers of sweat pouring down his back, he is the Allotment Holder-in-Chief, busy hoeing and fertilizing his world with all the vibrance, vitality and joy that he invests in every single life.

As we have noted often enough in the past, our special feast days always tally with the nature of his particular activity at certain times of the year and it is appropriate, then, that next Thursday is Ascension Day, one of the most important feast days of them all, if also the most misunderstood and least appreciated.

Ascension Day commemorates the day when Christ finally ascended in heaven. Forty days after the beginning of the huge drama of Easter Christ took his place at the right hand of God on this day and we can perhaps sense something of the awe the Apostles felt when they actually saw him going up into the clouds. Recollect the awe we all felt looking up at the Hale Bop comet streaming through the heavens and magnify that awe a thousand times.

He has gone, then, from the moment of the resurrection to a place of supreme power. He was not so much changing a place as undergoing a change of state. The transformation was not local or physical but spiritual and it was from heaven that, through the Holy Spirit, he continued to communicate with believers everywhere. As one Scottish theologian put it: 'The dust of the earth settled on the throne of the majesty on high.' From his throne he marshalled the Spirit to patrol over us.

So this feast day marks the time when Christ rejoined himself with the world and united himself with the ever-failing, stumbling story of mankind. He becomes its spirit, its genius, its source of energy and power. Our own story has finally taken on a central protagonist through whom everything makes a sort of sense, if only we actually believe in him. Ah, if only . . .

So stand and look at the skies next Thursday and, if you stare hard enough, perhaps you will see the hem of Christ's robe or his torn hands or bloodied feet moving up through the clouds like some ravaged comet in pyjamas trying to find its way home.

Alternatively, simply look around you and you will feel his universal godhood in the eyes of those marauding foxes, the brush of cobwebs on your cheeks, the cries of pain in the shadows, the sounds of distant storms threatening but failing to break . . . and everything else that lives and moves at the start of summer.

IRON ISLAM

There'll be a right old knees-up down in Cardiff's dockland this morning where, after a month of prayer and fasting, the Moslems will be ushering in their new year with long processions, hot curry and much general laughter.

Old Caradoc would need a lot more than a mere chicken

curry off-the-bone with a few poppadoms after a month of rigorous fasting like that but he's always had a soft spot for the Moslems and fully understands why such as Mike Tyson, Chris Eubank and even the great Mohammed Ali have run back into the welcoming and firm arms of this ancient faith when the going got rough.

Islam is no soft option like our present churches and chapels. Islam is a hard task-master with iron rules which demands much and takes even more. Every act of prayer is preceded by a careful and ritual washing and the faithful are expected to gather in the mosque every day for *zawya*: chanting and the settling of disputes.

All last month the Moslems would have learned about self-control and deprivation as they fasted from sunrise to sunset. They would have offered Allah their complete obedience and gone close to the poor and hungry. The closest we ever get to the poor and hungry is the odd bowl of soup whenever it crosses our minds about once every ten years – if that.

There are ten Mosques in Cardiff and the Moslems have become a great force in the commercial and cultural life of the city. I sometimes like to go down to the new one in Alice Street where the welcome is always cordial and the Imam has a thicker Cardiff accent than Frank Hennessy.

Here you can sit around waggling your stockinged toes to your heart's content as you look up at the beautiful dome with shafts of light breaking through the stained glass. 'There is no God but Allah and Mohammed is His Messenger,' it says on one of the windows.

This community has had its fair share of ups and downs over the years as when the local kids kept pinching their shoes when they were at prayer and flinging them over the rooftops. Shoes are not left out in the street anymore. There was another major row with the council when they insisted on slaughtering sheep in the street and upsetting the old ladies.

They also had a furious row amongst themselves about the siting of the old mosque in Peel Street which, it was alleged by some, didn't face Mecca. This row – which wasn't even resolved when they imported the biggest set of compasses and the biggest geographical brains in the world – has continued to this day and half of them still don't talk to the other half.

But they do live more or less amicably with everyone else, practising their beliefs in the absolute unity of God and the prophethood of Mohammed. They also take part in ritual prayer five times a day, alms-giving and undertake to make at least one pilgrimage to Mecca in their lives.

Mysticism also plays a large role in their faith and their main objective is a direct personal apprehension of God and a total submergence of self in the Divine. A regular study of the Koran means 'entering into a condition of peace and security with God through allegiance or surrender to Him'.

There is nothing at all wrong with any of this and if the chapel had managed to sustain their beliefs with a quarter of the Moslems' dedication and discipline, they almost certainly wouldn't be the spent and failing force that they have now become as the century draws to a close.

Deacons down on prayer mats, ritual prayers to Allah on the Big Seat, slaughtering sheep in the vestry... now perhaps there's a few notions for the chapel elders to conjure with. Or perhaps not.

FLASHES OF HOLY LIGHTNING

Picture a group of 120 praying in an upper room in Jerusalem. It is fifty days after the death of Christ and a hot day outside, due to get a lot hotter as the summer unfolds. The muezzin is making his calls to prayer in the nearby mosque and flies are buzzing around the sacks of spices in the market. The weird honkings of a hot and bothered donkey mingle with smoke from a charcoal grill. The mood in the twisting, hilly streets is strange and unpredictable.

Now something happens in that upper room which is not only going to have tremendous significance throughout the world but will even reach down into the twentieth-century Wales.

A great wind begins blasting through the still hot air over the rooftops of Jerusalem and our praying group looks up and around them. One man starts speaking in a strange and yet musical language which is unfamiliar to everyone else. Another joins in the rising babble with yet another language and then another and another. We have nothing short of linguistic bedlam; a raving UN without the benefit of any sort of translation service.

This eruption represents one of the first major lightning strikes of the Holy Spirit. This is the moment when all Christ's new followers have been given the gift of tongues and the modern church is born.

Tomorrow, the day of Pentecost, marks the anniversary of that strange and wonderful scene in Jerusalem. It is also the third greatest Christian feast after Christmas and Easter.

So, from that hot room in Jerusalem, we move to a little chapel in Loughour near Swansea in the autumn of 1904. There are but twelve in there, gathered after the normal Sunday evening service in the Moriah chapel. They are addressed by a young man called Evan Roberts and gas lights are hissing and puttering on the walls.

Everyone looks up at him expectantly as he says: 'I want each of you to say aloud in turn, "Oh Lord, send the Holy Spirit for Christ's sake. Amen."' They begin with this supplication which they make again and again.

This meeting will last until dawn. There are cries and visions. Some are struck down as if punched. Prayers come in strange voices and, by dawn, the first converts of a mighty revival leave the tiny chapel which is still there as it was on the fateful night. The Holy Spirit has struck again.

The influence of this Welsh revival in its turn leads to Azusa Street in downtown Los Angeles in 1906 where, amidst another blaze of Pentecostal passion and the speaking of tongues, the modern Pentecostal movement is born.

This evangelical and charismatic movement spreads throughout the world and is one of the few modern Christian groups that are actually growing with enormous power and confidence. It has also taken firm root in the House Church movement where they worship as if they actually mean it and pray in tongues.

Old Caradoc is always up for any such meetings which are often like taking a spiritual jacuzzi with lashings of Badedas after so many nights sitting in a zinc bath having your back scrubbed with carbolic in front of the fire.

Spontaneous prayers climb on the backs of isolated pleas.

Snatches of song can erupt too and everyone is more or less free to pitch in with more or less anything they might want to say in any language they might care to use. It is a form of Go-As-You-Please and often an exhilarating roller-coaster ride right into the heart of real worship.

So what happened in that upper room in Jerusalem continues to reach out to us to this day, and tomorrow of all days we should remember that the services of an all-powerful Holy Spirit remain at our call whether we choose to make that call in Pomeranian, Tamil or even Welsh.

THE DEMON DRINK

There was a preacher in America, the Revd Justin Edwards, who delivered his message with such fire, passion and conviction he became the foremost speaker of his day

Drink was the one rampant bee in Revd Justin's bonnet and he once delivered a sermon on the evils of drink which would have closed down Brains brewery overnight and which he later turned into a hugely popular Temperance Manual.

The core of his argument was that liquor could not be a part of the kingdom of God since it was not the product of creation, nor the result of any living process in nature. It does not exist in the living works of God.

But then Revd Justin really got down to it by listing the various drinks and diseases and punishments that went with them. There is, unfortunately, nothing about what happens when you drink too much Brains SA but punch, it seemed, brought idleness, sickness and debt. Egg rum earned you peevishness, tremors and jail. Brandy led to horse-racing, a red nose and the poorhouse. Too much bitters brought on stealing, jaundice and a dropping of every cavity in the body.

And if you thought all that was dreadful enough, be absolutely sure to stay off the gin – particularly first thing in the morning – since mother's ruin brought a whole dazzling display of punishments including perjury, dropsy, disgusting belching, palsy, murder, melancholy, a form of leprosy and the gallows. He didn't explain if you got any remission if you put lots of tonic in the gin.

It was religious fanatics like Revd Justin who finally conspired to bring about the social disaster of Prohibition in America, a subject we'll all learn a lot more about in a new BBC Wales series on television. Those thirteen years of Prohibition did America untold harm, contributing to a boom in crime and proving that the road to hell is indeed paved with good intentions.

The Revd Justin was full of good intentions, of course, and he won't be the first or last to ruin a good argument through monstrous exaggeration. Alcohol is one of the great destroyers and poisoners of our time but biblical teaching on it is unequivocal and clear: you may take alcohol but only in moderation.

Jesus performed his first miracle at Cana by changing water into the finest wine, and when it ran out he made some more. At the Last Supper he also began the practice of drinking wine in remembrance of his own shed blood. Wine, then, became the blood of the world and today when you look around you at the vineyards of France you can, it is thought by some, see his very spirit energizing the world.

Wine, we learn in various parts of the Bible, can gladden the heart, refresh the spirit and have a marvellous medicinal value. But we also learn again and again in those same pages that it can have a dark side, causing poverty and illness while also destroying both the understanding and the human personality. Both Noah and Lot went straight to the dogs after taking one too many.

Old Caradoc enjoys the odd snifter and he knows of many more who seem to benefit from the conviviality and fellowship that often come with alcohol. Beer, after all, has been the main lubricant of the minefields for more than a century.

But he knows of many more – and he sees them all around him every day – who have become literally imprisoned by alcohol and are living out Revd Justin Edwards' every dire prediction. See them now destroying themselves and their families, soon to be cruising the gutters with their health shot and nothing but rags on their backs and all simply because they ignored the biblical commandment to moderation.

ⵟWO NARRATIVES

All our lives, it is becoming increasingly clear from this pulpit, are being strung out on two narratives which are closely shadowing us and could even end up coming together and destroying us.

The first narrative is the story of our real lives from our awakening in the morning to that last moment at night when we lay our heads on our pillows.

There is usually no action or drama in this narrative: just the routine journey to work or around the house, the friction with the colleague on the next desk, the call of the gas man, the state of the canteen food, the dog urinating on the lawn, the boy in detention yet again and the thousand and one other moments that fill our days.

Pain will often seep into these days since pain is often the price we pay for loving too many people. We will often feel stress too, over a debt perhaps or a relationship that has gone sour.

This is real life in the real world: arid and pointless to many but full of drama and significance to a believer who will often, in the middle of the general gloom, find himself surprised by joy as when, say, the song of a bird will charm his ears or he watches the way light can fall on the face of a wild flower.

This joy is the special and unique gift of the Christian faith. In joy we often find the ability to handle our laughter and tears. Great music can bring us joy as can listening to the words of an inspired speaker. Christ said, 'No one can rob you of your joy.'

The second narrative is an entirely different story now being written through all our lives with many a loud explosion and knife thrust by the media. There is no truth or anything of our real world in this narrative since the media abhors normality and has no way of dealing with it.

Normality for the media is almost entirely based on crime, violence, terrorism, perversion, cruelty and atrocity of any kind. The dramatis personae in this narrative are gangsters, psychopaths, arsonists, joy-riders, murderers, terrorists and almost every other monster who is not only unlike you but entirely unknown to you.

But the awesome problem, it seems to Old Caradoc and

almost everyone else with half a brain, is that our second narrative, which is the embodiment of lies, is now having a direct bearing on our first narrative, which is the embodiment of truth.

The crime and violence of the screen are beginning to pour like rivers of acid into real life and, as it stands, it is our young who are being the most affected, many of whom have already been criminalized by this process from a very tender age. The young, the poor and the unemployed have always been especially vulnerable to the lies of the second narrative.

We older ones are perhaps not so easily influenced even if our normal lives are being undermined in a slightly different way. We are living with a growing fear about being burgled by our criminalized young. We worry about our bags being snatched or getting stabbed in a dark lane because we see it so often on our televisions and what we see on our televisions, programme-makers tell us repeatedly in one of their favourite lies, reflects real life.

Be in no doubt that one day soon these two narratives – already touching in places – will converge completely. The showing of *Reservoir Dogs* on Channel 4 has brought this day closer and we are going to have to take violent defensive measures when thugs talking and dressing like American gangsters burst into our homes threatening to slice off our ears. As they will.

As the narratives continue to intertwine, crime and violence will become a part of our everyday life. We will lose all sense of the normal and, where there was the quietness of a real life being lived next to real people, there will be a terrifying fear and, contrary to the promise of our Saviour, we will even be robbed of our joy.

GAY ISOLATION

I went on a bleak and pitiful pilgrimage recently to attend the funeral of a young man in a bleak and pitiful London suburb.

There were barely six of us there in the summer showers and we just stood looking at one another awkwardly before the hearse rolled up with a coffin unadorned by a single flower.

The service was over in less than 15 minutes and, with an organ rendition of 'A Whiter Shade of Pale', his all-time favourite, young Wilf was rolled down the castors into the crematorium furnace. Thus his short and painful life on earth was over. Wilf was a homosexual who died of AIDS.

I watched Wilf grow up in the Valleys and knew from the beginning he was not like the others. He was awkward, painfully sensitive and always hanging around in the background of things. The family was troubled and there was the biggest row ever when he was once caught trying on his sister's dress. I tried to befriend him and we had the odd chat but, perhaps predictably, he didn't have much to do with the chapel which has always seen all sexual activity – outside the missionary position within a heterosexual marriage – as a sign of insanity. Soon he knew – but never accepted – the nature of his condition, once seeking me out and asking, in the strictest confidence, what God made of homosexuality.

The Bible does tend to take a jaundiced view of it, I explained, but the prophets never really saw it as important and, anyway, the key homophobic jibes in those pages were derived from a faulty translation of the original Hebrew.

But he could be certain that the very heart of God was love and he did not fall outside that love because of some problem with his genes. All his life Christ was surrounded by prostitutes, deviants and gangsters but he never condemned or judged them.

Young Wilf wasn't convinced but it wasn't chapel which drove him out of the Valleys in the end so much as the troglodytic Valley folk themselves who, undoubtedly because of the chapel, have always reacted to homosexuals with unremitting disgust if not downright fear.

He went to Cardiff for a while before moving to London where, I heard through gossip, he'd found a form of happiness without having to deal with bigots on every corner. He even once sent me a nice postcard from Brighton with a view of the pier.

But he contracted HIV which, in turn, led to full-blown AIDS. He got so small they could have buried him in a shoe-box in the end, they said. His final weeks were but a snivelling, scabrous pain until his death and a funeral in Kensal Rise.

I was the only man from Wales there to say farewell to a man who had been damned to a life of loneliness and exile by our unreasoning outrage and bigotry. He deserved more than our disgust while he could also have done without the juvenile exhibitionism of the so-called gay groups now so vociferously screaming for acceptance in the church and other institutions. We will only come to terms with this painful, complex subject when both sides start learning the virtues of silence on it. The more silence the better.

No one represented that shrivelled young man in that coffin with any dignity and he had a lonely, unmourned death followed by a lonelier funeral. Even the vicar conducting the service didn't seem to know anything about him.

God always takes pleasure in our love wherever – and with whomever – we may find it. He wants us all to have quality relationships in which we find the treasures of long-term companionship and emotional security. The path of love is the only path and following this path doesn't mean elbowing aside people whose sexuality we disapprove of. We all elbowed aside young Wilf – even those who claimed to speak for him.

Our SUMMER HEARTS

We are well into summer and, as usual, I have often found myself sitting on a river bank with my trousers rolled up and the cool water flowing over my carbuncles, staring into space and trying to hold a prayer of praise in my mind.

The essence of summer is the way that water works in the soil and we can then watch and wonder at the result: whole fields of marvellous growth, the drifting scents of the trees and, of course, the flowers themselves standing around in gaudy and thrilling display.

With everything furiously blossoming and fruiting you can all but see the very soul of the earth rising up in a state of ecstatic longing towards the sky. Streams and eddies of life are everywhere feeding into this rising soul just as the moral life of man drifts through the perfumed breezes. These are moments of pure joy, the frequent consolation and reward of the believer.

You might even in such moments, if you were very lucky and caught the light in the right way, spot a summer angel or two tending the odd human heart. Angels particularly like working within huge rolls of summer sunshine and this is an especially good time of year to examine the state of our own hearts – as they are often referred to in the Old Testament – or our consciences as they are more commonly called in the New.

Such sunshine hours give us a literally golden opportunity to look at that strange concept of our conscience which, Christians agree, is unique to man. This conscience is the capacity for judging the rightness of our actions and some fine philosophers like Berkeley have even argued that it is the first sign of God in man.

Our consciences are our personal navigational lights through the present storms of terror, doubt and darkness that are threatening to engulf us. They are the internal mentors who will always show us the right path when we might be presented by many complex routes.

For that German rationalist Immanuel Kant, the conscience was an awareness of the universal claim of the moral dictates of reason. We should act in a way we would expect everyone else to act, he said. This was the Categorical Imperative and, for him, the existence of conscience was one of the first proofs of the existence of God. It was conscience, then, that sets us apart from animals and can even be seen as the mediator between the Law of God and the will of man, if not the voice of God himself.

Modern philosophy has tended to define the conscience as an internalized moral habit but modern philosophy went straight to the dogs the day the logical positivists took over and has never really found its way home again. Not only was their philosophy up the wall but their lives were a total shambles too. You would generally get more sense out of talking to one of my carbuncles than you would talking to your average logical positivist.

So it is good and right, then, to find your own place on a river bank in this splendid summer of ours and, with the water washing your feet, have a good chat with your conscience which might well be the nearest you will ever get to an intimate conversation with God.

Take up your problems with your conscience like, say, that woman you are sleeping with who you shouldn't or that money you stole or even how, generally, you are getting on with your children. Put the case honestly and carefully before yourself and then listen to what your conscience tells you.

Merely follow what is right and you may well regain your equilibrium in a difficult time or even come up with a new path which you might not otherwise have thought of. You might have to face up to a lot of pain in following the path of rightness but, in the long term, it will work out fine. It will, it will.

Visions of Death

It was a bad, strange day full of bad, strange weather and I felt a sense of persistent menace almost from the moment I woke up, riven with pain, at odds with everything and badly needing some spiritual support.

On such old devil days I will often repair to my derelict chapel, sitting quietly in the corner on one of the dusty pews where I can often revive my spirit by listening to the sounds of some of the great old chapel meetings of the past.

Occasionally God will talk to me through the dim burble of distant sounds and it is a rare day when I don't leave my chapel feeling a good deal better that when I went in.

But not on this bad, strange day of mine. Oh no. There was nothing at all in the chapel air except cobwebs and the cold. I heard a low and harrowing groan of pain coming out of the walls and even got the sense of a thick and slimy darkness gathering in the rafters.

I left quickly, walking down to the river bank only to find that here the water had blackened just as it had once been in the days of coal. Fish floated in the foul stench belly up. Frothy dark clouds spat cold drops of rain and even the marauding sheep, never exactly white, looked like massing black demons out to start trouble.

The plants and vegetables in my allotment seemed to be withering and dying too, so all that was left to me was to raise up my arms and turn and turn again in this land of encroaching evil and darkness. Just what was happening to us?

Old Caradoc has felt the closeness of evil all his life but he never expected it to spill over with quite such intensity or pure malevolence.

But isn't there a sound biblical reason for all this darkness and decay? The Bible teaches clearly that natural evil is the consequence of moral evil. Sinless man went into the Garden of Eden, disobeyed God and was kicked out again. Thereafter man was condemned to bring forth the fruit of the earth and the woman the fruit of her womb — in darkness and pain.

This view is sustained throughout the Bible. Job finally understands that he deserves his suffering because of his own sinfulness. The prophets talk of a coming Messiah who is going to lead us back into a Garden of Eden. The evil in the world will not be able to harm the true believer who will not only find himself in paradise but will be fully protected there.

But now we have all been vanquished from paradise, my wild, dark visions seem to be telling me. My people, who now routinely disobey every single law of the God of their ancestors, have let loose a flood of evil which is eating right at the core of every home and family.

Evil has always lurked deep in the waters of the world, ever ready to make an appearance, but now its face seems to be on permanent display to those with the eyes to see. See it in the needles in the playgrounds, the empty alcopop bottles, the smashed-up bus shelters, the blood left after fights, the shrill domestic rows and the broken families . . . everywhere the detritus of a faithless people who have broken their historic covenant with God.

God did not create evil and neither did he make us robots. He gave us guidelines for living and, most crucially, the ability to choose between good and evil. In choosing good we are made happy. In choosing evil we have become the unhappiest of the unhappy, never smiling unless drunk, forever squealing about the injustices of the world as we stumble from pub to betting shop and divorce lawyer, unable to find a single guiding light anywhere in this valley of growing darkness.

𝔄 HIGH TIDE OF EVIL

One of the highest tides for years swept up on the beaches of Cornwall and South Wales last week due to the peculiar conjunctions of sun and moon.

I went down to take a look at it late one night and, glazed by moonlight, the brown waters of the Bristol Channel looked distinctly menacing, the tide full with its own mystery, the bracken and other rubbish washed up high on the shoreline, the barely perceptible suck and wash of the small waves on the cracking pebbles.

There was an awesome power in that sea, a massive and yet unrealized ability to turn violent at any moment and destroy everything it came near. Just one wild wind and all the furies of the world would have been released.

The high tide of human evil is now flowing at record levels too and we are all up to our waists in it, waiting nervously for that one wild wind to stoke up the waves and sweep us all away.

It is lapping around our hearts and homes, planting scabrous nightmares in our minds, destroying our belief in the family, feeding our voracious prurience, criminalizing our young and even, on occasion, openly attacking and killing our loved ones like Princess Diana.

Should you disbelieve any of this and should it sound like the lonely rantings of an old man in an old pulpit, then look at the mounting evidence now swirling around us like that moonlit flotsam.

Look at the Royal Academy and the present exhibition, Sensations, which, according to the organizer, is a show for this moment in English history. Well, it is certainly that with a head made from the artist's own blood, a portrait of a bullet hole, mutated children engaged in perverted sex, cut-up animals, quartered sharks and its undoubted masterpiece, a portrait of Myra Hindley made from the handprints of small children.

I can hardly believe I have written the last paragraph, let alone that it is a description of an exhibition in the Royal Academy. Anyone who feels moved to throw anything at all these paedophilic fantasies has Old Caradoc's full and unqualified support. Hey, fling a few for me.

This show mounted – as you might well imagine – by a rich Tory twerp is a naked and open display of a face of the evil which has become such a menacing feature of all our lives.

Such art tells us little about God's creation and a lot about the cancerous visions of the modern artist. It shows how completely the artist has lost his way and how, unable to resonate with the real world and help us see and understand it, he is now peddling his squalid and sick nightmares.

Such grotesque and life-denying trash was not confined to the Royal Academy last week. In the new film *Nil by Mouth* we are shown a woman 'kicked to a bloody pulp on the floor'. In another new film *Face* we have another extended advertisement for ram-raiding, thieving and criminal violence. But, unless we miss the point, don't forget the director was really trying to show how bad all this was.

The Lakes on BBC1 presented us with the real lakes of the North as we have never seen them before – with more copulating couples on their slopes than sheep – and there was a most unusual shot in *Holding On* since the camera was actually down the pan filming a man vomiting on it.

Understand that modern artists have all infected one another with these viruses and that they are suffering from a sickness unto death. Further understand that your loved ones are under constant and vicious attack.

Find a lifeboat of true faith, my people, since soon now – perhaps sooner than anyone ever expected – a wild wind is going to blow across this high tide of evil which will indeed rise up and destroy everything it comes near.

MYSTICAL AUTUMN

I was walking down a path, revelling in the magnificent colours of an autumnal afternoon, when a few leaves fell on my head, tumbled off my shoulder and landed at my feet.

I lifted my eyes and squinted at the brightness of the sun as it broke through the overhanging branches. There were still a lot more leaves to fall but those few lying at my feet released a sudden stream of ideas, sounds and images.

The sound, which lifted as suddenly as a quick wind, was of the first line of that great harvest festival hymn: 'We plough the fields and scatter the good seed on the land . . .' and I was back again, standing in front of a chapel altar piled high with fruit and vegetables, giving thanks for the abundance of the earth.

Spiders worked in webs patterned with drops of dew. Flowers were making their last defiant and colourful gasp. Tomatoes were brilliantly red as the plant itself withered. Rotten apples had been drilled hollow by wasps.

Death was racing here and there over the brown bracken and boulders of the Valley, killing off everything that grew in preparation for a long winter of sleep. As one season ends, then the next always begins; this is the cycle of day and night, the very rhythm of the earth.

Everything in the natural world dies with the outbreak of autumn yet, in this death, we ourselves find new reserves and willingness to carry on. The life of the human spirit asserts itself as we move forward into the bleakness of winter.

We do not die like nature but move forward another year. The glories of our own bodies take longer to die but die they will. To the dust we will all return.

At the centre of these mysterious cycles of life and death, which closely mirror and shadow one another, stands Christ. He met a widow carrying her dead son for burial at Nain and said: 'Young man, I say unto thee arise.' The young man who had died in the full fruit of his life lived. Christ's words gave him new life and blood.

So in these infinitely sad days when the leaves fall and the voluptuous dream of summer turns into the damp quietness of autumn, we should be able to see and understand many of the strange and mysterious forces which underpin our lives.

We should see and understand that only Christ can give us new life when the rest of the world is filling with death and decay. We should see and understand that, as one existence closes and opens up for another, then we also continually teeter on much the same cusp and, while autumn may not signal death for us, this season does bring our own end that much closer. Death is the one inescapable and unavoidable fact. Even non-believers can't get around that.

And there in death through Christ – and only through Christ – will we find a resurrection in the coming spring of love. This is what it means to be human; this is what it means to be a part of God's fruit of the earth.

These are all lonely, mystical thoughts, I know, but autumn is a lonely, mystical business. It is a turning point of mists which does not make obvious sense. Life is taken away so that it can be given back again. We die that we may live again.

And so it was with the singing of 'We plough the fields and scatter . . .' still ringing in my mind and with a dazzle of sunlight still in my eyes that I picked up those few dead leaves at my feet and walked on my way.

GORGEOUS GEORGE

How many stabs in the heart can an old man take? I was still reeling from the death of Diana, then came Mother Theresa and, still trying to come to terms with my scorched feelings, I lost my good friend George Thomas.

He was a prince among men was George; someone whose spirit will inhabit and haunt the Valleys forever. I doubt there will ever be a day when I don't actually think of him.

We had shared a number of times of prayer together and his faith was as solid as the Dowlais Top. In fact the only time he had ever doubted his faith, he once told me, was after his beloved Mam died.

We were politically on the same side as well and had a friend-ship lasting 40 years. I visited him a few times in his Speaker's Flat in the House of Commons where he positively effervesced with jokes and pleasure at the way everything had worked out for him.

But he was very much a man waiting to die after his retire-ment to his bungalow in King George V Drive in Cardiff. He had received all the world had to give, he felt, and there was no bitterness in his heart now that the end was near. God had given him a marvellous innings.

What was he really like? Well, I'll tell you. With his thin, laughing features and great conk; with his infectious optimism and funny sense of style he always put me in mind of a square-dance fiddler, hammering away on the stage of a barn while smiling, always smiling at the sound of his own stunning virtuosity. In many ways he was as simple as a raindrop and just about the most loving man I've ever met.

His love of his Mam was as great as any heart has ever been capable. He took her everywhere with him; referred to her constantly in his speeches and she even had a slot in his election pamphlets. 'My son George will never let you down.' Her death devastated him and he never really recovered from it.

His relationship with Harold Wilson was always good-natured. George bullied him one day about a glass of brandy he had spotted on his desk. 'Oh leave me alone, George. All I want is a glass of brandy.' One day, late at night, he spotted Gwynfor Evans in the House. George put his arm around him. 'What are you doing here, Gwynfor? Why don't you go home to your family?'

He never got on with Crossman whose cruel and savage remarks about him wounded him to the core. But his one great ace in the hole was his wit which marked him out as a real survivor.

When asked why, as a wartime policeman, he never arrested anyone, he said: 'The war will soon be over and I'm going to have to live in this community. I believe in cautions.' When one rowdy backbencher in the Commons shouted 'It must be true because it's in the papers', George replied: 'Yes, and so is my horoscope.'

He was enormously proud of being Speaker and, on one wall of his flat, he had his own coat of arms, featuring a coal miner's lamp, a daffodil and a leek. All around were portraits of other Speakers, including his own. 'That's Sir John Trevor there. Jailed for corruption he was. You'll see he had a squint so no one knew who he was looking at and they had to start calling Members by name.'

These were the happiest times for him but, I thought, he

never quite shook off his inherent loneliness, particularly after his Mam went. There were sides to him that we will never know about but that's as it should be. We should all be allowed to take our little secrets to the grave.

One of the principal arguments for the existence of God lies in the evidence of the lives of ordinary men. George was an ordinary man who constantly mediated the idea of God to us. He was a Methodist beacon, a Welsh light in a modern darkness, a generous gift from a generous God to us all.

LANDSCAPES OF PRAYER

I have known many strange and savage hours of inner struggle this autumn, sitting alone in my pew in my derelict chapel and trying to come to terms with the darkness deep in my soul. These hours of prayer and meditation begin, as ever, as I sit there looking up at the cobwebbed pulpit while trying to clear my mind of every thought and image.

I have long learned that I can only begin such journeys in a clearing when I can then move forward, in quiet prayer, picking up whatever insights I can. These hours are set aside for my personal pilgrimages into the very heart of God. Sometimes they are successful and replenishing but, of late, it's all got rather hopeless.

I keep getting pulled back by dark hands on my journey. The earth keeps disappearing from under my hesitant feet. Then, a few times now, I have broken my face against a high dark wall and I have just stood there, with my nose bleeding, moving my palms over this wall which is as high as it is unyielding. What is this wall and why is my progress across a landscape of prayer being blocked in this way?

Then, in that moment of blinding clarity that we often get when we first awake, I understood that this high, dark wall was myself. Here with a bleeding nose Old Caradoc had been confronted and repulsed by himself.

It began making a sort of sense. Those clinging hands were thoughts of myself. The loss of the earth under my feet was the loss of my faith because I had become so preoccupied with myself. That high, dark wall was nothing less than the giant Himalayan range of my own ego beyond which I could go no further.

This high dark wall of the self must stand at the very centre of our lost and fallen condition. Everything that is evil and rotten about us is sprayed like graffiti on that wall – our unbridled appetites for money, sex, power, fame, possessions . . .

Look up at your own wall now. Note the Lottery tickets and condoms fluttering in the barbed wire. See the advertisements for new cars and televisions. Oh, look at that beautiful new home. But notice this very special feature: see all these mirrors embedded in the wall here and there so that, when you look in them, you can see the wonderfully entrancing image of your own face. At this wall you can gaze at the face of your own selfishness forever!

Stand back a little, Sir, and survey its sheer size as it towers over – and controls – you. Oh yes, this wall really is what your own prison looks like and, until you get out of this prison, you will never be free. You will never, ever savour the deep secrets and lasting satisfactions of real freedom.

On this wall we break our noses on our own self-love. Here we shrivel in a total eclipse of the sun as we pick out the winning numbers of the Lottery in our absurd fantasies. Here whole families are destroyed as we abandon our children and run off to other beds in pursuit of better sex. Here we lie and cheat and steal. Here we study our horoscopes anxiously and hope for a change in our luck. This is a place of valium and vibrators from which nothing of any use will ever emerge.

We must, I believe, do nothing less than break the control of this self-will over all our lives. We must move beyond our own base appetites and self-indulgence. We can only ever become free again if we root our lives in that which is eternal and absolute; that which is beyond ourselves.

The only and certain way to truly crucify your ego is to surrender to the words and spirit of Christ. He alone offers us the ladder by which we will be able to freely negotiate that high dark wall of ourselves so that we can then run free again and back into the welcoming and loving arms of God.

𝔐AGICAL ASHRAM

Something truly extraordinary is going on up the end of a rutted track and in a low spin of damp hills in the chapel heartlands of West Wales.

For here, not far from the birthplace of one of our greatest pulpit-shakers, Christmas Evans, a group of young people are doing nothing less than busily re-writing the spiritual history of Wales.

A friend took me there recently since, he said, it was something I should know about. This turned out to be true and the place is indeed something that everyone should know about. Glorying in the wonderful title of the Community of the Many Names of God, this community of around 16 full-time brothers with changing numbers of helpers and led by a real Indian guru, have set up an Indian ashram which is not only Hindu but also Buddhist and Christian.

They are based in two far-flung farmsteads, with one on top of a high hill, in which they have built two amazing temples complete with gold domes. They believe that God has spoken to all the major religious prophets and so their services, which begin with a pooja at five in the morning, vary constantly as they use Hindu prayers, Sanskrit verses, Buddhist chants and Christian hymns.

Old Caradoc attended one of the midday poojas in their new temple, standing at the rear in his socks as one of the brothers led the chanting and held up a flaming lantern which burned purified ghee (clarified butter) which he kept circling in front of an effigy of Lord Subramium. (You must stand at the rear if you have eaten meat, eggs or milk in the previous three days.)

I must say I enjoyed it all immensely and came away feeling I had been at a real service. We were even invited to wash our faces in the flames and I always wanted to have one of those strange dots in the middle of my forehead. Also I've never had any problems with other people's religions. All religions are true and we are all made in the image of God who is at work in everyone.

Certainly, the work of this ashram is nothing short of stupendous since not only do they support and value all forms of animal and human life but they are also now setting up a hospice nursing system throughout the area, even providing accommodation for the voluntary nurses in another farmhouse which they have recently bought. Terminally ill people, they believe, should be allowed to die at home in comfort and surrounded by their things.

They also have an extremely pampered, if not downright spoilt, Indian elephant, Valli, here who has just been built a new compound where she sometimes trumpets or shows off to visitors. They don't let her roam around because she then starts trying to push down trees.

They also have llamas, given to them by a farmer on the verge of going broke, peacocks and any number of stray dogs free to wander anywhere they like. The gardener, Gwyn Williams, is not even allowed to kill slugs in his cabbages and he used to tell people he takes them over the other side of the stream since slugs can't swim back to his cabbages again. He has, however, just discovered that slugs can, in fact, swim underwater, so now he lets them get on with it.

One interesting rule of the ashram is that they never talk to the media who have, on occasion, savaged them quite badly. They rely on donations.

All this is the brainchild of one of the most charismatic men I have met, known to all as the Guru, an amusing and even inspiring Indian with sparkly black eyes. He is very nearly blind but says he sees everything with 'a visionary eye'. He knows everything in the Bible but has never read it. He only eats a small piece of roti each morning and a spoon of rice at night. 'God gives me all the energy I need.'

The Welsh always tend to run away from what they don't understand but they should embrace the work of this brilliant and unique Indian with his visionary eye since, from the vantage point of this pulpit anyway, he is just about all we've got.

DYLAN THOMAS DAY

I caught a small news item in *The Western Mail* the other day and looked up into the eye of a startling and terrible vision of Wales, certainly the most startling and terrible vision of Wales that Old Caradoc has ever beheld.

The new item suggested that there should be a Dylan Thomas Day and there, in this vision, thousands of schoolchildren, wearing curly Dylan Thomas wigs and long scarfs, were wending their ways to school, swigging on flagons of bitter, spouting rubbish and all at least an hour late.

Normal lessons had been abandoned for this new Welsh holy day and the subjects on offer this morning were How To Sponge Off Other People; The Easiest Ways To Abandon Your Wife and Children; A Dozen Good Ways of Dealing With A Hangover and The Art of Writing Effective Begging Letters.

The school day ended earlier than usual with a special assembly in which the finalists were announced for The Most Incomprehensible Line Written For An Alcoholic Voice. Each of the finalists got up onto the school rostrum, complete with curly wig and long scarf, to read, in a mock Oxford accent, their most meaningless and pointless lines. Competition was intense and the laughter unconfined.

'Out of the singing black whiteness a taste of ice cream death makes its way to the crow-haunted abattoir,' said one. 'I am the sugar cuckoo who pinches the Bible-black nest of my star-gestured neighbour,' another chimed in. 'Give me the first slow-worm hour in the dung-infested dawn and I will serve up loads of mindless rubbish on warm toast,' also received loud applause.

All schools had a half day on this great new day with every pupil sent home with a bottle of Guinness which had been painted the colour of a daffodil. Once home the pupils joined their families who, even at this early hour, were all already on their way to getting as drunk as wheels. Many of the fathers greedily and cruelly grabbed those yellow bottles of Guinness, guzzling them down as their children sobbed.

A diversity of events took place in the afternoon. There was a competition to see who could steal the most items from the homes of their neighbours and ferry them to the local pawn-shops. Another competition was set up to see who could vomit the furthest without splashing their shoes after drinking ten pints of bitter.

A special rugby match was also staged in St Helen's, Swansea, when every player was expected to cheat and break every rule in the book. Each of them had to be at least twice over the limit before they got onto the pitch and any side, in this state, which managed to wilfully and successfully mislead the referee had their score automatically doubled.

Anyone who did a stroke of work on this day was judged a traitor to Wales but, if you really did have to do something – apart from lifting a lot of heavy glasses or filling in a few betting slips – then, of course, a spot of energetic adultery clearly fell within the spirit and meaning of this new day of total self-indulgence.

In the evening everyone who was still conscious met in the pubs and, over yet more gallons of drink, spoke to one another in red-eyed gibberish. Everyone laughed. Everyone cried. Everyone wet themselves. Come midnight the English came over the border and scraped up the comatose Welsh out of gutters and ditches to take them home in wheelbarrows.

Oh aye, this was a great new day in the Welsh calendar all right. The national emblem became a pink elephant. The anthem was played backwards. All flags flew upside down. Every thief, adulterer and drunkard had become a national hero in his own right.

But maybe, on second thoughts, we're all right as we are with St David's Day, celebrating a good man who worked hard, spoke clearly, drank only water and didn't rat on everyone he came near.

STARTLING SERMONS

The art of delivering a sermon popped up into the news twice last week, albeit with one appearing in a happier light than the other.

They had a sort of sermon shoot-out in the mighty Durham Cathedral for the Speaker of the Year Award while, in America, a preacher admitted he had prepared a sermon while under the influence of crack cocaine. I am not suggesting these two news items are in any way related and am certainly not aware of any-one in a Welsh pulpit who has ever tried to preach the word of the Lord on crack cocaine.

Old Caradoc has heard a few who have *sounded* as if they have been on crack cocaine but, generally, our ministers seem to have taken time and trouble with their words, even if they are then delivered on a Sunday morning to six old ladies and a tin of salmon.

It is not much of an exaggeration to say that the very soul and conscience of Wales was pounded out on the anvil of the pulpit by the hammer of the sermon. Indeed, there was a time when the pulpit was the heart of all social life; the centre of all poetry, philosophy and drama.

A first-class sermon was defined as having the power to enthral and subdue; there had to be a well-ordered development of the argument from a sound premise to a rock-solid conclusion and, wherever possible, this argument should be continually decorated by interplays of humour and irony.

It was also expected that the whole congregation should stay awake for its duration. 'If a man is going to sleep in my congregation don't wake him up, wake me up,' said C. H. Spurgeon, that sparkling Baptist.

The preacher himself was also expected to be the supreme intellectual who could take apart the logical positivists with deft argument as well as show us which end of the pen Socrates used for his discourses. The preacher challenged, he provoked, he pounded his poor old pulpit, sometimes in anger at the stupidity of what he saw.

Some of us actually cowered in our pews as he stood there speaking of the blasphemous daring and unmitigated insolence of those Roman soldiers in their rough handling of the Son of God. On occasions he might get into the *hywl* with his voice bellowing like an organ stop. You would swear that he really was trying to punch a hole in the bottom of hell.

But then he might take up the scalpel of softness and precision as, like a surgeon, he sought to cut out a social habit which he saw as opposing the mind and laws of God. His general aim was to preach as a dying man to dying men, unfathoming the mysteries of Revelation with the thunder of Sinai. His was a forensic pleading for the saving power of the Christian faith.

He could go on a bit, it was true. Some of his best sermons had been heard again and again for twenty years yet, somehow, we seemed to enjoy them more and more every time they were delivered. There were those mock-theatrical double takes and pianissimos, by now as familiar to us as the rain on a winter Valley Sunday. And the long silences. Who could every forget those long silences?

He might even have borrowed another minister's sermons, slowing down – or so the old story goes – to read the note in the margin: 'Argument a bit weak here. Shout like hell.'

Go and listen to your local preacher again next Sunday and listen again to the voice of the pulpit. These preachers did nothing less than make and save us. Watch out for the old stories too and the mannerisms and the double takes. But whatever you do, don't smile too much if they start shouting like hell.

ℭHE DESTRUCTION OF LIES

I was having a chat with a divorce lawyer recently and the thing that really depressed him about almost all his clients, he said, was that they told him lies. Even at the point where the relationship had fully and finally foundered, with the ritual arguments about children and money going on, his clients still kept telling him lies, usually about the existence of 'someone else'.

In matters of sex and love, it seems, we can never tell the truth. We always want to conceal what is really in our hearts and, for all kinds of reasons, keep telling lies about it, often in some misguided effort not to hurt our partners or children.

'When they say no one else is involved, I have to try hard to contain my laughter,' said my lawyer friend. 'This is the one great lie of our time along with the one about your cheque being in the post. Interestingly, the bigger the liar, the more he often suffers in the end. The truth will always catch up with even the most accomplished liar in the end.'

This man seems to have across an absolute truth which Old Caradoc commends. Lies poison all our relationships absolutely. The lie is the rock on which the ship of marriage is now foundering. Lies are deadly viruses which eat through every corner of a relationship, always leaving it dead and rotten in the end.

As soon as you begin lying to your partner your relationship is already starting to come apart whether you know it or not. In one way I suppose it makes some sense when you go on to start lying to your lawyer too.

A relationship will only ever work on the basis of honesty and I have seen many a 'lost' marriage make a miraculous recovery when one or the other finally introduces an element of honesty and tells the truth, usually about the much-denied existence of someone else.

Continual lies muddy the issues and make a healing impossible. The liar is a menace to everyone including himself; he destroys that bedrock of trust without which any relationship is pointless. Another problem is that you require an exceptional memory to be a good liar and few have that.

So if you are reading this in bed on a Saturday morning and your marriage is in trouble because there is something you are concealing and are telling lies about it, then tell your partner everything. Make a cup of tea first, take a deep breath and spew it all out.

There'll be trouble and pain for sure but nothing like the trouble and pain that's coming down the tracks. Yet even after an hour of this trouble and pain your relationship will already start mending and keep on mending in direct proportion to the amount of honesty you keep pouring into it.

Hold nothing back. Tell the truth, the whole truth and nothing but the truth. The amount of forgiveness your partner does show, in the end, might astonish you. Heads will start clearing themselves of small mysteries. The relief will be immediate and real.

Truth is a therapy in itself which also has an inherent loveliness. It is also one of God's most abiding and refreshing qualities. Job told us we should never tell a lie for God. 'Speak truthfully of your neighbour because we are all members of one body.'

So hold up the flame of the truth and always live by its light. It is the only possible light by which your relationships can grow into a mature and happy fruitfulness. Lies will corrupt and destroy. You cannot live a lie.

Only in the pleasing light of truth will you ever manage to raise your children to be happy and successful. This is our only real duty in these fractured and difficult times – that we do what is best for them and only then will we be able to put our hand on an honest heart and say 'Yes, I did the decent thing.'

A DEADLY PAIRING

It seems barely credible that, after failure upon failure, the Church is still trying to get a foot into television. The Church seems to think there's a future in this chaotic world with all its chaotic imagery.

The latest candidate for a quick bankruptcy has come in the form of the GOD Christian Channel launched last week in Sir Terence Conran's fashionable Mezzo restaurant in London.

It will be sharing a satellite frequency with Sky soap and sci-fi channels and I hope they settle down and become happy with one another. But like all the other evangelistic enterprises on television, including the ill-fated ARK in Bristol, GOD won't last long.

The bare truth of the matter is that the Church and television make a deadly pairing with what goes on in one actively hostile to what goes on in the other.

Television is an essentially atomized and aggressive medium which portrays a world which is fragmented, superficial and discontinuous. Millions of images are pouring out of it constantly and most of them barely last 3.5 seconds. Murder, Ron Davies, rape, the Welsh Assembly, angry farmers, *EastEnders,* crocodiles . . . the whole sorry lot of them come pouring down on us in fleeting pictures and addled sound bites.

This chaos is inimical to a religious sensibility which values such things as order, argument, meaning and meditation. But advertisements on television actually swamp anything like that; they are for brightness, glitter and the *now.* Any feeling for the sacred is always destroyed by banality.

'The danger is not that religion becomes the content of television shows,' wrote Neil Postman, the American media commentator, 'but that television shows may become the content of religion. God does not play well on television.'

The electronic church, as seen on American television, has become a woeful place of blatant commercialism and exposed hucksters. The communion was between salesmen and their gullible purchasers. The confessional was replaced by a computerized tape. There was a theme park which looked like Jerusalem. This church, which was not a church, had traded in the cross for a television aerial.

Old Caradoc believes the Church will again become a powerful platform for Christian witness; the Church will again become prophetic but the timing of this will be the gift of God alone and certainly not Rupert Murdoch's.

Television, far from being an arena for God, has become the main arm of the opposition, continuously pouring out beatings, murder, rape, perversion and crime which do not in any way mirror real life or the ordinary world.

Television keeps telling us lies merely by being what it is and even the American chat shows with their 'nuts and sluts' are pouring out sleaze throughout the afternoons with not one of them being a person you or I might know. Everyone on *EastEnders* is barmy, with not one of them acting like a civilized human being who knows how to talk to one another, except that nice new priest who might get hung up on the Christmas tree in the square by Christmas Eve.

But the main point here is that evangelistic television simply does not work. I've never known anyone converted by television although I've known many who have picked up some extremely nutty ideas from it. The Church should not add to this chaos but seek alternatives.

Jesus never appeared on television or on a game show or spoke into a microphone. But his words still ring as blazingly true today as when he first broadcast them, merely with his mouth and to the sunshine on the shores of Galilee almost two thousand years ago.

BEATING BURGLARS

There was a hell of a rumpus around our way the other night

when one of the many apprentice burglars we all seem to be rearing so carefully these days was caught stuck in a front window.

It sounds like something out of a Buster Keaton film, I know, but there he was half-in and half-out of a woman's front parlour where the window had dropped down on him and he was flailing about like some giant maggot in shell suit and trainers desperate to catch the attention of a passing fish.

The only attention he did catch, as it turned out, was that of the 61-year-old woman he was trying to rob. This woman, a most mild soul with a fondness for tapestry, came down the stairs in her nightgown and duly proceeded to beat the living daylights out of her burglar with a carpet cleaner.

She walloped him so much you would have thought she had just finished a 12-hour shift watching video nasties and, oh boy, did her burglar howl and howl. He was covered with bruises by the time she had finished and she only did that after the neighbours intervened worried that she might kill him.

He limped off in the end, howling with bruises and swearing he was going to get her. But it was all mouth and he won't be coming back. His father was also told what had happened and he duly beat the boy up all over again. Certainly his burglary career seems to have come to a premature end and, perhaps fortunately, he didn't get near the police or our wonderful social workers.

I'm not sure why I found this small story of crime and punishment so pleasing although I did some biblical research and discovered that in Babylonia a householder catching a burglar in the act could have him executed and walled up in the breach he made. The mind boggles at the estate agent's description: this attractive property comes with the new insulation of many compacted burglars, guaranteed to scare off any other burglars for ten years.

Punishment in biblical times was as rigorous as it was often complex and you get a clear feeling there wasn't too much crime around. Often it was 'an eye for an eye' although the less developed the culture (as with the Assyrians), the more savage the punishment. Murder and kidnapping were always punished by death. Among the Hebrews an offender whose assault caused a permanent injury suffered an identical injury as a punishment.

Damage to property was punished by fines or restitution.

Rape was punished severely – if it occurred out-of-doors the rapist was put to death and if it occurred indoors they were, for some obscure reason, *both* put to death.

If a son was found guilty of persistent drunkenness a father could stone him to death – which wouldn't leave many sons in the South Wales Valleys these days. Adultery was punishable by stoning and any crimes against the King also warranted death by arrows or the gallows. Physical punishment included being beaten by rods or scourges. Many punishments were undertaken by the nearest living relative of the victim, thus some form of revenge was involved as well as possible clemency.

In biblical times crime was seen as a rejection of God and all his holy laws. A criminal broke the covenant between a deity and a community; in so doing he was also inviting retribution on the whole community.

So we can see another reason why we are all staggering and slipping in this modern blizzard of lawlessness which is threatening to sweep us all away. We have lost our nerve to punish and our criminals know it. We no longer have any feeling for – or conviction in – a strong moral or legal code. We are even, heaven help all of us, allowing a Minister of the Crown to go into the Maze Prison in Northern Ireland to talk to convicted murderers.

This is another side of our faithlessness. We were once punished for it by such as boils and locusts. Now it's murder, violence and robbery without end.

A COMING IN ICE

The Valley slumped into its usual torpor after the Christmas explosion with icicles hanging off the gutterings of the terraces and families sitting around the front of their televisions for hour after hour. What did we do before television?

There is an almost savage beauty about the high volcanic walls in these strange, cold hours. Frost seems to jewel the rocks and, as the rising sun strikes the one side of the Valley, you can actually watch the frost disappear even if it never seems to lift from the dark side.

Occasionally the sheep change slopes, looking for a bit of warmth as they cross the river which runs along the Valley floor where the pebbles keep changing colour and the brown trout dart from beneath one rock to another.

No one was out anywhere when I walked up to the end of the Valley the other morning. You couldn't hear anything either as my boots crunched into the puddles of ice and my warm breath plumed around me dragonish.

Here and there water had worked loose beneath the ice on the rocks and the wriggling drops looked like giant tadpoles trying to break free. Olive pellets of fresh sheep dung were piled up here and there. An old pram lay on its side in the river.

You can still spot the black patches of the old tips through their ragged coverings of ice and grass and I always, without fail, remember the final days of the last miners' strike when I am out this way. Hundreds of villagers were out here digging for lumps of coal in the old tips and they had the poetry and serenity of a routed army about them. Life was going to go on somehow. It was the time of the greatest triumph of our collier spirit which, in its turn, led to our betrayal and most bitter defeat. They just left us to die in the end.

They have even taken away the mine workings now, filled in the shaft and grassed the lot over. Everything has gone – the washery, the changing rooms, the numerous drams . . . and, looking at this uneven cricket pitch, it is difficult to picture the dark geometry of that old hole again, even in my memory.

I walked on towards the end of the Valley where a few diehards were fishing in the riffling waters of the reservoir. I have never understood fishermen and always think of Dr Johnson's quote when I see them: 'A fool on one end of a line and a worm on the other.'

Then I came close to the final high wall and had the feeling, as I looked up and around me, that I was walking down the central aisle of a nave of a cathedral sculpted out of cloud and ice. The high rocks loomed over me and, with a tremble of some distant but beautiful chords, I heard the music of the tribe coming up out of the very earth.

I cannot tell you what this music was but it was the saddest, most unbearable, most heartbreaking oratorio of anguish I have ever heard. This was the powerful lament of a tribe who had lost its way. It spoke of death in the family and the way that even the angels had deserted us.

The anguish of this tribal music invaded every part of my being and, shaking with its sadness, I took off my hat and, with head bowed, waited for it to stop. But it didn't so I decided to walk straight into it and up to the High Altar of that final Valley wall.

This terrible music stopped when I finally sank to my knees. Prayers swept around the choir stalls of the rocks. The sun caught in a patch of snow making it sparkle briefly like a bank of votive candles. Two blackbirds flew overhead and there was the single toll of a deep, dead bell.

Then I looked up high and it was as if my very blood had stopped flowing since mine eyes were filled with the glory of the coming of the Lord.

A bearded man with a long white robe was standing alone on top of the slope. He held out both his hands towards me when, with a further sparkling swirl of sunlight across ice, he was gone. Gone, gone, gone, gone, gone.

HINDING GOD IN US

I was standing quite still the other night, gazing up into a vast and beautiful field of stars when I began asking myself why many of us have such a small concept of God. Everyone has a few ideas about him and that is the real trouble. These ideas are few, thin and generally stupid. Rarely is he presented in a vast vision of a field of stars with his crucified Son set in the middle of this great and glittering night sky.

Old Caradoc was taught thin things about God in Sunday School and the chapel. He also worked out the skeleton of God from the Bible but never quite knew anything about him until, one day, he began putting the flesh on the skeleton himself, creating him in his mind and, from that moment, this act of personal creation never quite stopped.

So I built him out of the rubble on a pilgrim path and the

memories of all the people I have loved. He took shape in the ashes of my dead mother and that moment I stood at the altar on my wedding day. He came to life in a Snowdonia sunset and the sweat of my brow as I built my first home with my own hands.

I caught sight of him in the beautiful eyes of innocent children and in all the good men whom I have met and who changed me. I alone created him out of the sunlight in the morning and the darkness of the pit; out of the clouds and the rain and the vines of the field.

I clothed him in the daily miracles of an ordinary world; in the intricate patterns of a wild flower; in the smell of woodsmoke from a garden fire and in the song of all the birds that greet every dawn. I bathed him in the tears of my people after Aberfan and my own tears after I had lost those I loved and in the hurrying waters of the River Taff, clean again now that all the mines have closed. I fed him with my very blood just as he continues to feed me.

I met him in the kitchen as I was washing up the dishes and found him in the fiery glow of a coal fire and the marigolds in the garden and the dishes on the Welsh dresser. He rustled through all the movements of the house and came specially close when the cat got up on the back of my armchair and licked my bald patch.

It became that he was everywhere I turned, a ready comforter to the frightened trembling of my heart when I was stricken with despair or fear. He became a vital part of me, someone who was always there, ready to talk to me when there was something I really needed to hear, built by me out of all the leaves in the forest and the dust of the earth, out of the quickening pulse of the morning and the refreshing of a good sleep.

I came to live in the very heart of him and, when I went down on my knees to worship him, I was worshipping life itself. He had become my controlling force and I had been made happy.

You too should create your own God in your own way who will serve and help you just as he serves and helps me. Take whatever you have found to be honest and beautiful and good. Feed your mind and heart on it and soon you will find your way out of the darkness that enfolds you.

Remove those satellite dishes before it is too late, my people, since everything that comes out of them is a black rain of sex, horror and violence. This black rain will, in its turn, fertilize the Devil himself inside you whose greatest joy will be to reduce your life to rubble as you squeal in misery and despair.

Let the fragrances of goodness and truth blow through your hearts so that you might live again and be free. Wash away your pain with the clean rain of heaven. All you need to do this is to build a God of the good and small things. Forget the Church and create him for yourself out of whatever is in you, out of whatever is lovely in your life, out of the wild poetry in your wayward Welsh hearts.

Afterword

Caradoc would like to thank Simon Kingston and Alison Barr at SPCK for anthologizing his sermons, and Peter Jones, Carolyn Hitt and Neil Fowler of *The Western Mail* for their unstinting support. But there is only one woman who completely holds his ailing frame together with the daily glory of her love – Mrs Caradoc – and it is to her that this collection is prayerfully dedicated.